The Trogglybogs
of Brinscall Moors

This story is dedicated to all the people who, for centuries, lived and worked on the moors. They would have toiled hard and their quality of life would inevitably have been poor.

The Trogglybogs
of Brinscall Moors

ALEC PRICE

To Ashley & Jack

Best wishes

Alec Price

⚞ Moorland Publishing ⚟

Brinscall

Published by Moorland Publishing
21 Chapel Street, Brinscall, Lancs PR6 8QD

ISBN 978-0-9549895-1-4

First published 2007

Edited and typeset by
Frances Hackeson Freelance Publishing Services, Brinscall, Lancs
Printed in Great Britain by
CPL Design and Print, Preston, Lancs.

Acknowledgements

My thanks to my nephew Stuart Roberts for his computer expertise, to my very good friend Joan Appleton for her time and patience, to Eileen Briscoe for her amazing artwork, to Frances Hackeson for editorial work and last but not least, to my granddaughter Chloe, for her inspiration.

Introduction

I was for many years a keen walker, and did most of my walking on the moors above Brinscall, both because it was easy to access and because of the sheer beauty of the hills. Those moors also hold a air of mystery about them.

All over the hills on the West Pennine Moors there are the remnants of a civilization that died out well over one hundred years ago. Cottages and small farmhouses (all now in ruin) are dotted around the hillsides. The roads that once would have been the main routes for farmers and travellers are now nothing more than spidery tracks that walkers use as they go along their rambles.

It is the evidence of these houses from the past that suggest the moors hold secrets, secrets that only the stones know, and stones can't speak of what has gone on centuries before ... the centuries before the farms and cottages became derelict.

Whenever I walk upon those hills I sense something, whether that something is just the peace and quiet I don't really know, but it's as if I am not totally alone. It is a feeling of being watched. Once when I got this same feeling, I stopped and looked around to see if I could see anyone, but all I saw was the head of a grouse popping up and down in the long grass. It was as if it was watching me.

It is strange, but all books that are written about moors are written by people who have often walked the hills, and they will all tell you the same thing. The moors are places of mystery and beauty – especially mystery! Perhaps it wasn't a grouse watching me after all?

1

The Adventure Begins

James Breaks had been told of a small herd of roe deer that had moved onto the moors just below Great Hill. His excitement got the better of him; he decided he would have to investigate.

It was a mild if somewhat miserable sort of a morning in late April when James set off in search of his quarry. He wrapped up well, making sure he packed his waterproofs, knowing only too well that the weather could change at the drop of a hat, especially up on the tops of the moor. It took James about an hour to arrive at the lower reaches of Great Hill and as he did he wondered if the weather would stay fine. The low cloud was drifting across the moor, brushing the tops of the higher hills as it passed over them.

Right on the top of Great Hill was a stone wall that had been specially erected for walkers to sit behind and rest out of the wind. The hill was about 1,200 feet above sea level and when the wind blew up there, boy, did it blow! When James finally arrived at the wall he decided this was a good time to stop for a break. Sitting down, he took out his thermos flask and sandwiches.

As he did the mist that had been threatening to descend onto the moor, did just that. 'Oh well, no chance of spotting any deer today', James thought to himself. Sitting there with his tea and sandwiches, he was deep in thought, mainly thinking how peaceful and tranquil it was all that way from civilization. On a clear day the view from the top of Great Hill was breathtaking. In one direction was the West Pennine Moors with Darwen Tower standing proud in the distance and, looking the other way, it was possible to see the mountains of the Lake District.

Suddenly, James's peace was disturbed by the sound of laughter. At first James thought it was children, but it wasn't like any children's laughter he had ever heard before. 'Great', he thought, 'that'll scare the deer off.' He was about to stand up to have a better look at what or who was making all the commotion, when he noticed a stone missing out of the wall.

James leaned over for a peep and what he saw shook him to his very bones. Before him, playing in the long grass, were two of the strangest creatures he had ever seen in his life. They were both about two feet tall with large elf-like ears and they were covered from head to toe in long brown hair. He stared at them for a moment, watching them playing like two normal

children, except these certainly were not children. Although they looked like some kind of monsters, they sounded and played like ordinary children, even speaking English!

James reached for his rucksack, and grabbing his camera he stood up and aimed his lens in the direction of the creatures, but before he could take a picture, they had disappeared – vanished!

'What the … where did they go?' James couldn't see them anywhere. Had he seen them at all? He sat down, in shock. Was it the mist playing tricks with him? No, it couldn't have been. He had heard them as well as having seen them. 'I wonder …' he thought to himself.

In the village of Brinscall there had always been a kind of story about the Trogglybogs; 'mysterious creatures' that lived on the moors. Most people treated the stories as a folklore joke, although some had claimed to have seen them. However, those who had said they'd seen them, were said to have been either drunk or crazy! James wasn't in either of these categories, so what had he seen? Was it really the Trogglybogs of Brinscall Moor?

Quickly he packed up his things and headed off home; he had to tell someone what he had seen and his wife would be that person. Hurrying all the way back over the moors, sometimes almost falling over through not watching where he was going, his eyes were scouring the heather and the hills for any more signs of these mysterious little creatures. As he reached lower ground the mist lifted and this caused him to look even harder, but there was nothing, just the odd bird fluttering about in and out of the grass to break the silence.

The walk across the moor to Great Hill had taken James over an hour, but he reached the top of the lane that leads off the moor in half that time. His excitement and the urge to share his experience with his wife had sped him on. Ten minutes later he was walking through his front door.

'Anna, Anna', he shouted.

'What on earth's the matter – are you all right?' asked Anna in a concerned voice.

James began to tell Anna what he had seen on the moor.

'For heaven's sake, slow down and calm down; you're going to burst a blood vessel!'

'Anna, you must tell me, do you know of anyone who has seen the Trogglybogs, or says they have?' asked James.

'Well, there is old Harriet Bond who lives down by the crossing, she used to say that she was their friend. Everyone said she was mad, but I always found her to be a nice old lady … I haven't seen her for ages, but she still lives there as far as I know. Why don't you go and speak to her?'

'Will you come with me? I don't know her, but she might remember you.'

'Oh, very well', said Anna.

'C'mon, we'll go now', said James.

Anna looked at her husband as if he was demented: he was normally a very easygoing and calm person. She also realized that whatever he had seen on the moor that morning must have been for real. This behaviour was very much out of character for her James.

They put on their coats and set off to Miss Bond's cottage. It was a fair walk down the long tree-lined lane and past the big Hall. The lane past the Hall was an unmade road and only one cottage was down that road … Miss Bond's.

'Why on earth would anyone want to live down here on their own?' asked James. There was nothing down there apart from the old disused railway track.

On one side of Miss Bond's house were fields and on the other side a huge wood. James found just walking past the Hall a somewhat spooky experience; he certainly wouldn't like to live right down at the bottom of the lane where Miss Bond lived. James and Anna arrived at the gate of the cottage. Pushing Anna forward, James held back. The cottage was very old; ivy grew all over its walls and in the garden large trees overhung the house, making it very dark. Anna knocked on the heavy wooden door. After a while a voice enquired from the other side, 'Who's there?'

'Miss Bond, it's Anna Breaks. Do you remember me? I have my husband with me … can we speak with you for a moment?'

One by one the bolts on the door clunked, before it slowly opened about six inches to reveal a security chain. From behind the door the frail figure of the little old lady peered at the two visitors.

'Ah yes, I do remember you,' said Miss Bond, 'what do you want?'

'Miss Bond, my husband would like to talk to you about the Trogglybogs. He thinks he might have seen them on the moors today. Can we come in?'

Miss Bond slipped the chain off the door and opened it.

'Come in, come in', said the old lady in an excited voice. 'Would you like some tea? I was just putting the kettle on'.

'Thank you', they both replied in unison.

After a few minutes Miss Bond appeared from the kitchen carrying a tray with tea and biscuits. Placing it down on a small table at the front of a big open fire, she then sat down in the most enormous armchair. She looked like a tiny doll.

'Will you be mother, dear?' asked the old lady.

Anna poured the tea and James began to tell Miss Bond what he had seen that day on the moors at Great Hill. The old lady laughed out loud, and clapped her hands with excitement.

'At last! At last someone has seen them. I once told someone I'd seen them you know, but people think I'm just a silly old woman, they said I made up the stories – but I didn't'.

'How well did you know them? And where do they come from? Are they aliens?' asked James.

Miss Bond laughed. 'No of course they're not aliens, silly; they're just children, but very special children.'

Settling down in her huge chair she proceeded to tell James and Anna all she knew about the Trogglybogs of Brinscall Moor.

2

Harriet's Story

When I was a little girl – I think it was when I was about ten years old – myself and a few friends had gone to play in the woods. Normally, we would only go as far as the waterfall, but this particular day for some strange reason we went right to the top of the wood, where it leads onto the moors. We climbed over the wall and went onto the moor itself. I'd never been beyond the woods before and I thought it was very exciting.

After we had been playing for a while someone suggested we have a game of hide and seek. We took it in turns who should seek. When it came to my turn I searched everywhere for my friends, but when I couldn't find them after about twenty minutes I began to get upset – I later found out that they had sneaked off home for a joke!

Anyway, I sat down and began to cry. To make matters worse it got very misty and I didn't know how to get home. I was terribly afraid.

Suddenly out of the mist appeared two very odd-looking creatures, about two feet tall, with large pointed ears and covered in long brown hair, just as you described them.

'Why are you crying?' one of them asked me.

By now I was even more afraid: I had never seen anything like these two creatures before and I didn't know if they were dangerous or not.

'Don't be afraid, we will help you', said the other one.

They spoke perfect English and it was clear by their voices

that one was a girl and the other a boy. I explained that my friends had run off and left me and that I didn't know my way off the moor.

'That's OK, we will show you the way … but it will cost you some sweets', said the boy.

I told him I didn't have any sweets with me, but I promised him I would return with some another day. At first he sulked, and then he started to smile.

'Very well, but you must come alone and you must not tell anyone you have seen us', said the boy. I asked him who he was and where he was from. At first I found it very hard to believe what he told me – and so will you! He said that he and his friends had lived on the moors since the year 1602.'

James let out a huge gasp. 'Never in this world – that's four hundred years – impossible!'

'I said you wouldn't believe me! The boy went on to tell me that one cold November day in 1602, an old woman had been crossing the moor from Pendle in the east to the market town of Chorley. It was a terrible day; the heavens had opened and the old woman had got cold and wet, her feet were bleeding and it was late afternoon. As she walked down from Great Hill, she saw smoke rising from a cottage chimney and decided to try and seek shelter for the night.   She walked round the side of the house and came face to face with Isaac Stanworth chopping logs. When he saw the woman approaching, he stopped, resting his axe on the block.

'What do you want, woman?' he demanded. 'There's nothing here for the likes of you. Be off with you or I'll set my dog on you!'

The old woman tried to explain that she meant him no harm and only wanted shelter for the night, but Mr Stanworth would not listen.

The woman tried at every cottage she came to, but no one would give her shelter that day. Even the coaching house would not let her sleep in the stable. The coachman said she was a witch and was evil. It turned out he was right. As the old

woman reached the top of the last big hill on the moor she could see the lights of Chorley in the distance. But closer than that was the village of Brinscall.

She turned back and looked in the direction from where she had come. As she did, anger welled up inside the woman and she let out a scream and a curse that echoed through every valley on the moor as it bounced off the hillsides. It sent shivers down the backs of everyone who heard it and filled them with fear.

'I curse you all who have turned me away this day. May all your children be taken from you and turned into Troglodytes ...

And may they be forced to dwell in the Bowels of the earth ... Forever!'

On hearing this all the parents ran to check upon their children only to find that they were all sleeping peacefully. However, the next morning, panic set in as one by one the families discovered that their children had disappeared.

That morning the farmers and crofters of the moor gathered and went in search of the old woman. They visited all the inns and hostelries in Chorley and the surrounding villages, but it was no good – she had vanished. For weeks, months even, the people searched for their children, but nothing was to be found of any of them anywhere.

Then one day about six months later, Samuel Rigby, a farmer was out on the moor tending his sheep and repairing a broken wall. As he was bending down doing his work all the sheep began to get agitated and then ran off as fast as they could. Mr Rigby looked around to see what had spooked the sheep but he couldn't see anything; he thought it might have been a fox or a stray dog, but there was nothing. Then he heard a voice call to him,

'Hello, father.'

When he looked over the wall in the direction of the sound, he saw two small hairy creatures standing there, smiling at him.

'Who are you? What are you?' he asked, shaking as he spoke.

'Don't you know us, daddy? It's us, your children Tommy and Lily', said one of them in a voice that he half-recognized.

That was the first time anyone had seen any of their children since that terrible night. It took a few minutes to convince Mr Rigby that these were indeed his two lost children. They looked so different with all the hair and they had grown huge bat-like ears, but there was no mistake, they were his children.

The two small 'Troglodytes' as the witch said they would become, explained that after they went to bed, the children thought they had all had the same dream and when they awoke, they found themselves in a large underground cavern by the side of a big lagoon. At first they were very afraid, but some of the older ones took control and reassured the younger ones that everything would be all right. Before long they set off through the labyrinth of tunnels and they found more and more caverns. In one of the caverns was a huge underground lake

11

that teemed with fish. Mushrooms and herbs grew in other caverns. But in the most amazing one of all they found the remains of Saxon warriors, including swords and shields and there were also bones! It turned out that they had fallen from the roof of the cavern; the hill above had been a Saxon burial ground.

Finding that cavern was the luckiest thing that could have happened to them. When they realized that the bones were from graves above, they set about reburying them in the cavern and they placed the swords and shields on top of the graves. After they did this they were about to leave when the whole cavern lit up and a deep voice called to them … 'Stop!' The voice told them he was the spirit of a Saxon chief and he told them they would be blessed with magic powers for what they had done that day. He told them that they would be watched over and protected by the spirits of the Saxons and that they would want for nothing.

'But what of the old witch and her terrible curse?' asked James.

'Well, it would appear her curse went wrong somewhere along the line that night, because they didn't turn into the fearsome Troglodytes that she said they would; but when she spoke the words "*may they dwell in the bowels of the earth forever*" it looks like she got the "forever" bit right. They never get ill and they don't grow any older. The only way they can ever die is if they are killed in a violent manner and some of them have been killed over the years. There were thirty-six of them in the beginning, now there are just twenty-four of them left.

'How did the others die?' James enquired.

'Most of them have been shot by people hunting on the moors, but when they die their bodies immediately turn to dust, probably because of their age. So the hunters who have shot them have never found the bodies. Because of this, it has never been proved that they exist.

The only knowledge of them is from people like you and me who have seen them and if you tell anyone that you've seen a

Trogglybog, you'll just get laughed at!'

'Where did they get the name "Trogglybog" from?' asked Anna.

'Well, after that first meeting between Samuel Rigby and his children Lily and Tommy, it was agreed that all the parents and their children should meet.

That was to be a very emotional meeting. There were a lot of tears and some very hard decisions had to be taken, but all the parents agreed; their children looked nothing like Troglodytes. Someone said they should become known as Trogglybogs because they lived in the boglands of the moor and they all agreed that Trogglybogs was a much kinder, cuter name for them than Troglodytes. Probably the hardest decision was that they would have to remain living were they were … in the caves.'

'I've walked over those moors for years and I have never ever found any caves, so where are they?' asked the totally bemused James.

'You never will find the caves; indeed the only way you'll ever be able to go down into them is if they take you down. The entrances are there, but they cannot be seen by ordinary people like you and I.

I remember Tommybog – that's my pet name for him – telling me of the day they met their parents and how they laughed when Dan Stone tried to follow his son into the caves. Harry – Dan's son, walked towards a big rock set in the hillside and like a ghost he walked straight through it and disappeared. Dan tried to follow his son by doing the same thing, but he was just met by a solid lump of rock and he ended up with a busted nose. Apparently everyone laughed, then Harry came back out, took hold of his father's hand and led him through the rock. All the children then took hold of their parents' hands and did the same thing. It's the only way ordinary people can enter the caves.

Another major decision that was taken was that no one should be told of their existence for fear of them being hunted down and killed. That was why they had to remain living in the caves forever.

After that first encounter, I met up with Tommy and Lily a number of times, taking them sweets and gaining their trust. It wasn't long before I was introduced to the rest of them and they took me down into the caverns. It is nothing like you would imagine down there. You would probably think it is dark, damp and cold – not so! It is warm, very dry and the caverns are lit by bright stones that shine like big diamonds embedded in the walls and ceilings of the caves. The lagoons are fresh water and teeming with brightly coloured fish. Food is plentiful, as thanks to their magic powers they can produce food from anything … they can turn soil into flour and rocks into potatoes. They can also communicate with all the animals of the moor – they're their friends! So they don't eat meat.'

'That's amazing; do they ever come here to see you?' asked James.

'No, I would never tell them where I lived; I always thought it would be too dangerous. Too many people pass by my cottage and I have always been afraid for their safety. If anyone were to see them, they would be in grave danger. It's a shame in a way, because I haven't seen them for over twenty years. My legs are far too old to carry me onto the moors now', said Harriet.

'Well, what if I were to go onto the moor and bring them down here to see you?' asked James.

Harriet laughed. 'And how do you propose to get them here? They're terrified of people, especially adults … they call adults the big people and they believe that the big people just want to shoot them – and in the past that has been the case so many times. I doubt you would have any luck even finding them again, let alone getting them to leave the moor.'

'Harriet's right', said Anna. 'Don't forget, you've been going onto those moors for donkeys years and you've never seen them before, so it's a good chance you might never see them again.'

'Every time you go onto the moor they will be watching you,

but you won't know they're there', said Harriet.

'Well, if that's the case, how come I saw them today?' asked James.

'You were just lucky today, you will probably never be that lucky again', replied Harriet.

'What if I was to go up there and shout out loud that I was their friend and that I meant them no harm? I could even take lots of sweets with me as a peace offering.'

Harriet smiled. 'You could try, I suppose, but I wouldn't bank your hopes on it working.'

'Well, I can't just give up, not now that I've seen them; I just have to try. So that's what I will do … first thing in the morning!'

James looked at his watch. 'Good heavens – look at the time! We've been here for over three hours.' James and Anna stood up, wished Harriet good night and thanked her for the tea and biscuits.

'If you do have any luck finding them, please promise me you will be careful who you tell; it could be so dangerous for them if the wrong people found out about them', pleaded Harriet.

'Don't worry, I'll tell no one – I don't want any harm to come to them either – it will be our secret', promised James.

As they left Miss Bond's house they smiled as they heard all the bolts and chains being fastened again. Neither of them could blame her for being secure, it was such a lonely and desolate spot where she lived.

Walking back up the long lane, James had a wonderful warm feeling inside him. The talk about the Trogglybogs had filled him with excitement. Even the sound of owls screeching as he passed the big Hall did nothing to dampen that warm glow.

'Isn't nature wonderful?' he asked Anna.

'It most certainly is', she agreed.

'I'm going to call in at the shop on the way home, to buy bags full of sweets for tomorrow', said James excitedly.

'You'll not sleep tonight, you're far too excited', said Anna.

On reaching the shop, which was just at the end of the road

where James and Anna lived, James went in and Anna carried on home. She decided to make some hot chocolate in the hope that it might relax James before bedtime. James soon came home, carrying half the shop.

'What on earth are you going to do with all that? It must have cost a fortune! You can't carry all that with you onto the moors – and what if you don't find them? You will have to bring it all back home.' Anna was furious with James for buying so many sweets.

'Calm down – they're not all for me, I've bought some for you for being such an understanding wife', he said with a smug grin on his face.

After watching television for a while and drinking his hot chocolate, James decided to go to bed. He set his alarm clock for six o'clock in the morning and settled down for the night.

3

The Search Begins

It took James over two hours to finally get off to sleep, as all he could think of was what he had seen that day, what Harriet had told him and what he was going to do the next day.

The following morning he was awake before the alarm clock went off, which meant it didn't disturb Anna – after all the last thing Anna would want to do would be to get up at 6am on a Sunday morning.

James got up and had a shower, making as little noise as he could. As he went downstairs he was greeted by his two dogs which had been asleep in the hallway.

'Sorry boys, it's going to have to be a quick walk this morning', said James.

Before putting his coat on and grabbing the dogs' leads, James switched the kettle on. All part of his plan for a quick and early start. He took the dogs to the field at the end of the road and let them off their leads. Off they ran, playing and barking as they ran. After five minutes, James called the dogs back; he wanted to be making tracks and he had to have some breakfast before he took off for the day.

Back in the house the kettle had boiled and James made himself a cup of tea and some toast. He also made himself some sandwiches and a flask of coffee to take with him. It was now nearly seven o'clock. He checked his rucksack to make sure he had everything he needed, including his stock of sweets. When he was sure he'd got everything he set off, giving his dogs a biscuit before going out of the door. 'I spoil those dogs', he thought to himself. Then he smiled as he thought of the goodies he was about to hand out to the Trogglybogs … 'Well, maybe not', he thought again.

After he had been walking for about half an hour he arrived at the gateway at the top of the road that led onto the moor itself. He hadn't really decided where to begin his search. He stopped for a moment, looking around. He wondered whether the Trogglybogs would even be up that early in the morning; looking around he saw that no one else was!

James made up his mind to walk over to Great Hill; that was where he had seen them the previous day and he might be lucky again, especially with having sweets this time, but he must remember what Harriet had warned him: he had been lucky and he might never be that lucky again. He knew he must not build his hopes up – after all, in twenty years of walking on those moors he had never seen them before.

After walking for just over an hour James reached Great Hill, heading for the same spot he had been to the day before. He sat down behind the wall. It was a much nicer day than yesterday had been and the sun was already quite warm even though it was only nine in the morning. The birds were singing and James was feeling very optimistic. He decided to spread some of the sweets out all around the wall. Then he had a good look around to make sure no one was about and he began to speak out loud.

'My name is James and I want to be your friend. I've brought sweets and chocolate for you. I mean you no harm; I just want to meet you.' James carried on talking out loud for quite a while, when suddenly from out of nowhere came a young man running over the moors.

'I doubt the rabbits will answer you back, mate', said the young man, laughing as he ran past James.

James hadn't heard the runner approaching and felt a right fool at being caught out talking to himself!

'Well,' he thought, 'if people are going to be running about here, I've no chance of making contact with the Trogglybogs –

why can't they find somewhere else to run?' At that point a group of hikers approached from the other direction.

James knew he had to find a spot where no one walked, somewhere off the main paths. He walked down off Great Hill and towards the deep gully that winds for ages until it comes out at White Coppice. He decided to cross the gully and go up the other side to Round Loaf Hill. This was said to be a Saxon burial mound and it was quite possible that it was the one Harriet had spoken of.

The hillsides and the gully were very steep; one slip and James could be badly injured and it would be unlikely anyone would come along that way and find him. The hill wasn't too bad to manage but the gully was something else. It was very deep in places and the water rushed down it with tremendous speed, it was about twelve feet deep, with rocky sides and quite wide in parts. James had to pick a spot where he could cross safely.

He walked upstream for a hundred yards before he came to a place that was shallow and quite easy. The water here was only knee-deep and there was the odd stepping-stone which was indeed a blessing. James didn't fancy getting his feet wet and having to tramp around in wet socks all day.

Once across, he had to begin the climb up to the top of Round Loaf Hill. After about fifteen minutes he reached the top, very pleased with himself, but then realized he had to repeat the whole process when it was time to go home. James stopped for a moment and looked at Round Loaf Hill. It was a strange-looking place, some one hundred yards across and a perfectly rounded mound, rising to about twenty feet high in the middle; it was easy to see how it had become known by its name – it looked like a large green teacake.

'I wonder why people say it is a Saxon burial mound?' James thought to himself, 'Has anyone ever done any excavation work here?'

Once again James decided to try and make contact with the Trogglybogs. He took out his sweets, laid them out on the ground, and began to speak in a loud, clear voice. 'My name is James and I want to be your friend. I mean you no harm. I have brought you sweets and I am a friend of Harriet … I just want to talk to you.'

James repeated this every two or three minutes, but… nothing! After a while he took out his thermos flask and sandwiches and had his lunch, it was now 1.30pm. It was a lovely day and the spring sunshine was quite warm. James thought, 'Well, I don't know where you are, Trogglybogs, but I hope you're out here somewhere enjoying this sunshine.'

James lay back and relaxed, and before he knew it he had fallen asleep; the warmth and the peace and quiet had proven to be too relaxing. James awoke with a start and looked at his watch – 3.20pm!

'I had better be heading back', he thought. He got to his feet and was about to pick up the sweets he had earlier spread out for the Trogglybogs but there weren't any – they had all gone. James looked at the sheep that were grazing close by.

'Do sheep like sweets?' he wondered, 'or have the Trogglybogs paid me a visit while I was asleep? How strange!'

As James stood there looking around, he had a funny feeling that he was being watched, but he couldn't see anyone or anything … except the sheep. He wondered if they would be so cheeky as to take the sweets while he was lying there. 'Surely not', he thought. 'I will have to ask Harriet – if anyone will know, she will.'

After collecting his belongings together, he began to make his way down the hillside. He had only walked a few yards when a flock of big black crows flew over him, all of them carrying sticks, and like aircraft on a bombing raid they dropped the sticks all around him, some of them hitting him as they fell. Then they made a huge racket and flew off down the gully in the direction of White Coppice.

This frightened James a little. Was it a warning from the Trogglybogs to keep off their patch? After all, Harriet had told him that they had magic powers and that they were friends with all the animals of the moors. James made his way down to the gully and found the place where he had crossed earlier. There were no further signs of the crows, thank goodness.

Once across the gully James walked home still feeling as if he was being watched all the way, but he could see nothing. The afternoon had brought a lot of walkers out onto the moors. The small birds that seem to flit in and out of the grass were busy going about their business and the odd kestrel hovered on the wing looking for its lunch. It was a beautiful place to be on a Sunday afternoon and who could blame all these people for coming up there to enjoy it. Although it didn't help James's quest to track down the Trogglybogs of Brinscall Moors. He may not have made contact with them, but he was pretty sure those crows were connected somehow.

About two hundred yards from the gate that leads from the moor, James saw a fox walking along the edge of the wood, beneath the wall. It stopped and watched James as he made his way down the last few yards of the path to the gate. James opened the gate and went through, and as he glanced across, the fox appeared to nod its head up and down before running off in the same direction it had come from.

This set James thinking. Was he now becoming paranoid? looking at everything and reading something into the situation – something that probably had no connection! He made his mind up: he would have to pay Harriet a visit to see what she thought of these strange happenings.

James arrived home at a quarter past five, just as Anna was laying the table.

'Well, did you see anything?' she enquired.

'Not exactly, but I did have a few strange experiences. I was bombed by crows and followed by a fox, well, more like escorted by a fox!'

Anna looked at him, puzzled.

'I'll explain over dinner', he said.

James proceeded to tell Anna everything that had happened that day. By the time he had finished she was in hysterics. She could imagine the runner thinking James was talking to himself, the crows dive-bombing him and a fox giving him the evil eye.

She did agree with him that it was all a bit peculiar, especially all the sweets disappearing while he was asleep.

'I must admit I have never known sheep to be lovers of sweets – maybe it was the crows!' said Anna, laughing again.

'Very funny. Well I'm going down to see Harriet to see what she makes of it.'

James finished his meal and took his dogs for the walk he had promised them earlier. He returned an hour later and sat down, exhausted.

'I think I will give Harriet's a miss tonight – I'm shattered! I'm getting too old to be walking up and down those hills, especially like I have today, off the beaten track.'

'Good idea', said Anna. 'They will still be there tomorrow; if they've been on those moors for four hundred years they'll wait another day to be discovered, I'm sure!' she added.

James yawned. 'I think I'll have an early night, it's work tomorrow. I think I might even put in for a holiday … I'm due one.'

Anna agreed with him and told him to go up to bed; she would lock up and switch off all the lights.

4

The Box

James was up for work at his usual time of 5am. His mind, as he drove to the bakery that morning, was not on the job in hand, and as he pulled into the car park it dawned on him that he could remember hardly any of the journey into work. That was bad! All he had thought about was his weekend and his encounter with the Trogglybogs.

He went straight in to see his boss. Stuart, the bakery owner, had been a good friend for over thirty years and had been his employer for the past seven years, but James knew that he couldn't tell Stuart the real reason why he wanted a holiday. He hated having to lie to his friend, but under the circumstances it had to be done.

'Morning Stuart, how are we this morning? enquired James gingerly.

'We are fine, but I can tell you're after something … Don't think of asking for a rise, I've just had to pay the tax man a fortune.'

'No, it's nothing like that', laughed James. 'But I could do with some time off, and it is about eight months since I had a holiday'.

'Yeah that's OK, it's pretty quiet at the moment. Are you going away?' asked Stuart.

'No, I just have one or two things to do at home and I could do with the time off.'

All that day at work James's mind was on how he would find the elusive Trogglybogs. He couldn't wait to begin his search. While he was working he came up with an idea that might just work, but he would have to ask Harriet first.

On arriving home that night he told Anna of his brainwave and she agreed he would have to speak to Harriet. After tea, James and Anna set off to go to Harriet's house, taking the two dogs with them for the walk. All the way down the lane the dogs were running in and out of the rough scrubland that was on one side of the lane, occasionally chasing the odd squirrel or rabbit, but never catching any.

When they arrived at Harriet's cottage James tied the dogleads to the fence and knocked at the door. Harriet had seen them coming and was already unbolting it.

'Hello Miss Bond', they both said.

'Is it all right to leave the dogs here? They'll be very quiet and hopefully we shouldn't keep you too long', said James.

'Yes, you can leave them there … just so long as you don't want to bring them inside – mother would never have dogs near the house, she was more of a cat person – hated dogs!' replied Harriet.

Once inside Harriet insisted they have tea and off she went into her kitchen to make it.

'Would you like some biscuits?' she asked.

'Oh no thank you, we've only just eaten', said James.

As soon as the ritual with the tea was over and Anna had again been asked to be mother, James told Harriet of his day on the moors and his encounter with the crows. Harriet laughed.

'It certainly sounds like the kind of prank the Trogglybogs would get up to, and as for the fox, that would definitely be them keeping an eye on you. I think you did make contact even though you didn't see them', said Harriet. 'They will know that you're after them now and no doubt they will be keeping a very close eye on you every time you go onto the moors', she warned.

'I've come up with an idea, but it's up to you as to whether or not you'll agree to what I have in mind. You might think it's a silly idea, but I think it's a good one', said James.

'Well, let's be hearing it', said the old lady, who was by now getting a little impatient.

'OK. Do you think that if they heard your voice they would recognize it? Bearing in mind that they haven't seen or heard from you for so long', asked James.

'Yes I'm sure they would, but there is no way I could go up onto those moors now at my age ... I'm sorry!'

'That's not what I have in mind. I've brought with me my tape recorder, now if I could record your voice and play it back – out loud on the moors, there's a good chance that they would know it was you and they might just respond to hearing you. What do you think?' asked James.

'I think you're daft, but I'll try if you want me to.'

James took out his tape recorder and switched it on.

'Just talk about the fun times you used to have with them when you used to go onto the moors, and call them by name.'

Harriet started by saying hello and spoke to them in a childlike manner.

'It's how I used to speak to them', she explained.

Carrying on, Harriet reminisced about old times and the things they got up to. After about twenty minutes, James stopped her; he could see the tears welling in her eyes and he knew it was becoming too emotional for her.

'That's fine', said James, putting his hand on hers.

'Yes, I'm sorry; it was bringing it all back to me ... All those wonderful times I used to have with my dear little friends ... I miss them so much!' said Harriet as she wiped away her tears.

The moment was broken by the sound of Bracken and Skip barking excitedly outside in the garden. James jumped up and went to the window to see what all the fuss was about. A cow had poked its head through the fence and was trying its best to eat the grass in Harriet's garden. Everyone laughed at this, which was good as it lightened the situation.

'It makes a nice change to have someone to talk to; usually I just have the animals for company ... I have a family of badgers that come foraging in the garden, my cat gets on very well with them and often plays with the cubs', said Harriet.

'That's amazing, I'd love to see them', said Anna, and James agreed.

'I think we'd better be going now before the dogs get any more excited', said James, passing Anna her coat, and giving Harriet a gentle kiss on the cheek.

'Tomorrow, I'll go back onto the moor and see if my tape recording of you has any effect', said James.

'I wouldn't get your hopes up, but good luck with it anyway', laughed Harriet.

As James and Anna walked down the path, the familiar sound of all the locks sliding closed worried James.

'Do you think she's all right, living all this way down here? What if she were to get ill? And no one knew. I wonder who her last visitors were before we started to come down here? She might not have seen anyone for months', said a worried James.

'I know that Peter keeps an eye on all the outlying cottages and farms. He told me that he gets well looked after with cups of tea and cakes on his visits.' Anna was referring to PC Hoyle, the village policeman.

'Well, that's good to know. I would hate her to come to any harm now that I've got to know her.'

Anna linked her arm through James's as they walked up the long lane back to the village. The huge cedar and sycamore trees that lined the lane gave the effect of walking through a tunnel as they overhung the road, blocking out the evening sunlight.

As they made their way back they passed Tom with his dog.

'Has he caught any rabbits tonight Tom?' enquired James, laughing.

'No, but there's time yet', replied Tom.

Tom's dog loved running about in the long grass and had caught the odd rabbit in the past. It had become a bit of a joke with the dog walkers who had seen Tom struggling with his dog as he tried to separate it from its prize.

When James got home he played the tape recording of Harriet. He and Anna thought it sounded good and James nodded his approval at what he had recorded.

'I just hope they do recognize Harriet's voice', he said. 'After all, if she hasn't been up on the moors for twenty years, her voice is bound to have changed.'

'I know, but there are things that she has said on the tape that only her and the Trogglybogs know about, so I think they will know that it's her – don't worry!'

James knew Anna was right, he just hoped that the Trogglybogs would come close enough to him to hear the recording.

'I had better run to the shop before it closes; I will need some more sweets for tomorrow.' James dashed out of the house and returned five minutes later with a carrier bag full of sweets.

'This must be costing us a fortune, and what must the people at the shop think?' said Anna.

James laughed. 'Peggy is worried; she thinks I'm buying them for the grandchildren. She told me off, saying I was going to ruin their teeth … if only she knew! I promised her I wouldn't give them to them all at once.'

Anna laughed; she could imagine Peggy telling James off in front of the packed shop and James having to lie through his teeth.

Sitting watching television, James couldn't help but wonder what the Trogglybogs were doing up there on the moors, or down in the caves. His thoughts were also with Harriet, alone in her cottage. Just over a week ago he had no knowledge of Harriet's way of life and he certainly had no knowledge of the Trogglybogs.

So much had happened in such a short space of time, and if everything was to go to plan, who knows what might happen tomorrow?

Anna was less excited about all this than James, and was beginning to fall asleep in her chair. James looked at his wife and thought how calm she appeared, when he was bursting with anticipation.

'C'mon … Bed time, I'll switch everything off', he said.

Anna went up to bed and James followed, even though he wasn't the least bit sleepy.

'Ah well, it will make the morning come quicker', he thought.

◁ 5 ▷

Sticks and Stones

As usual, James was awake before the alarm clock went off. He pressed the switch so it wouldn't go off and waken Anna. He crept out of bed and went to take a shower; after drying himself with the towel he went quietly back into the bedroom. He remembered being told by his sergeant when he was in the army cadets as a boy, never to wear any deodorant if you were going out to face the enemy. The reason was, because they would be able to smell you. Bearing this in mind James didn't apply his daily covering of Lynx. just in case the Trogglybogs smelled him coming. Not that he regarded them as his enemy.

Downstairs the two dogs were waiting for their usual walk, James grabbed his coat and the dogleads and off they went, heading for the field at the end of the road. Back at the house Anna had heard James go out with the dogs and had decided to get up. When James walked back into the house, a wonderful smell of bacon frying in the pan greeted him.

'You didn't need to get up, love', said James.

'I know you, it would have been a slice of toast and a mouthful of tea, and you'd have been off out. Trogglybog hunting! Well I want to be sure you have something proper inside you.'

'You're a gem, and no doubt', said a very grateful James.

Anna had laid the table and James sat down. He wasn't used to having a full English breakfast. Bacon, two eggs, tomatoes, mushrooms and fried bread, with toast, and a mug of tea.

'That should set you up for the day; breakfast is the main

meal of the day you know!' said Anna 'You can't go off walking all over those moors on an empty stomach.'

Anna was a lovely lady, and very caring. She and James had been married for thirty-two years; they had four children and four grandchildren. Heaven knows what they would make of his plans if they knew.

James finished his breakfast and gathered his things together, including the bag of sweets and a spare set of batteries for his tape recorder.

'You could always come with me', he said.

Anna gave him a look that didn't need any words to explain what she thought of that idea. James gave his wife a kiss and his dogs a biscuit; then slipping his rucksack over his shoulder, he was off.

It wasn't too bad a day, a bit cloudy but the weatherman had forecast a dry day and James was optimistic he would be right. It was half past eight and the tiny village of Brinscall was alive with people making their way to work and school. Down at the bus stop, two of James's grandchildren were waiting for the school bus. Kerry and her younger brother David spotted James.

'Where are you off to, Grandad?' shouted Kerry.

'I've got a few days off work, so I thought I'd do some walking – get a bit of the weight off', said James laughing and at the same time patting his tummy.

'Can I come with you?' asked David. 'I can tell the teacher I had to go to the dentist or something'.

'No you can't, young man, you'll get me shot!'

Just at that moment the school bus came around the corner. Boy, was James glad about that! David would have gone with him given half the chance; he was up for any kind of an adventure, any time.

Once across the main street it was just a few yards and James was on his way up the track that leads through the woods and up onto the moors. It was uphill for half a mile before he arrived at the gate that led onto the moor itself. The land levelled out once he got there and although it became rougher to walk on, it was easier. Looking back, the view from the top of the hill was magnificent. Brinscall was built on one side of a valley and on the other side were the woods and moors. 'It truly is a beautiful place to live', thought James.

He had made up his mind to he would head for the valley overlooking the gully, and there was one place just above White Coppice that was quite secluded and quite a bit off the main path. There would be very little chance of anyone stumbling across him while he played his tape. James also knew that this gully was where Harriet had said the Trogglybogs had met with their parents for the first time.

Half an hour later James was at the top of the path that led down to White Coppice. Before James turned down the path, he looked along the track towards Great Hill; about a hundred yards along were the ruin of the old coaching house. James wondered if it was the same one that Harriet had spoken of, where the old witch had been turned away. As he made his way down the rocky path he took time to stop and look at all the broken-down old cottages that were dotted about all over the moor. His thoughts turned to the people who would once have lived there; he also wondered if they were the same dwellings that the Trogglybogs parents had lived in. It saddened him a little to think that these moors were once a busy farming community, and now there was nothing left.

Soon James arrived above the section of the gully where he planned to try and make contact with the elusive Trogglybogs. Turning left off the path, he walked down through the rough grass and the long ferns. James walked down further until he was halfway down the gully. He stopped by a broken wall and sitting himself down on a large rock, proceeded to set out everything he had brought with him. He laid the sweets out all around him and put some of them on top of the wall, and then he took out his tape recorder and put it on the rock beside him.

'I think I'll have a nice cup of tea first', he said out loud to himself, half-hoping the Trogglybogs would hear him. James thought it would be a good idea to make a bit of noise, especially if, as Harriet said, they would be watching him every time he went onto the moors.

After he had poured himself his tea, he began to put his plan into action.

'Well Harriet, here we are then, no sign of your little friends … aren't you going to say hello to them?' James said in a loud voice.

Then he turned the volume of the tape recorder up full and switched it on.

Out boomed Harriet's voice.

'Hello my darling little friends, it's been a long time since I've seen you. How are you doing? I hope you're all well. Tommybog, do you remember the first time you took me down into your cave? How I banged my head and you made me better with your magic'.

Harriet's voice on the tape played for the full twenty minutes, but there was no sign of the Trogglybogs. James sat for a while and began to get downhearted. What was he meant to do?

He rewound the tape and began to play it again, and as it got to the end, just to the part where Harriet was beginning to get a little upset, James was struck on the back of the head by a stick … then another stick and stones were flying at him he was soon under heavy bombardment from all directions. Then the abuse started – he could hear shouting and yet he couldn't see anyone. He protected his head with his rucksack and curled up in a ball.

'Let Harriet out of that box, let her go, free our friend now … you'll be sorry if you don't'. The torrent of threats and the sticks and stones continued.

'All right … all right, just let me explain', pleaded James.

'No, let Harriet out of the box … now!'

'Please, Harriet isn't in the box … Honestly, it's a magic box … please just give me a minute to explain', pleaded James again. By now he was in serious fear for his life, and he was cut and bruised.

Then in an instant the volley of missiles stopped and the shouting subsided. James lifted his head from under his rucksack and for the first time he came face to face with the Trogglybogs of Brinscall Moors. There were at least twenty of them stood all around him, all of them still armed with hands full of sticks and stones.

'Right, you have one minute to let Harriet out of that box or we finish you off.'

James looked at the one who spoke and could see the anger in his face. Shaking, James began …

'Are you the one they call Tommybog?' James asked.

'No one but Harriet calls me by that name, now hurry, your time is running out.'

'All right, but you must believe me Harriet is not in this box, only her voice is in here … Let me show you how it works'.

With that they all became very agitated and began chanting in a strange language.

'It's all right honestly, here let me show you. I'll put my voice inside the box and then let you hear it, then if you want I will put your voice inside the box and you can hear yourself speak.' James quoted the nursery rhyme 'Baa, Baa, Black Sheep', and then played it back to his suspicious audience. On hearing this they looked at one another and muttered among themselves.

Tommy pushed one of the smaller Trogglybogs forward.

'Go on, speak to the box, and if it takes you inside we'll come and get you out', said Tommy, who was obviously the leader.

The poor unfortunate creature who had been selected was a young female.

'Don't be afraid', said James. 'I promise you, you will not go into the box, only your voice will ... trust me! I'm the only one in danger here', said James.

'Right, my name is James. What's your name?'

'Lily', replied the girl.

'Very well, Lily, you're Tommy's sister, aren't you? And your father was Samuel Rigby', said James. 'I know all this because Harriet is my friend and she has told me all about you.'

James then rewound the tape again and played it back to the amazed gathering.

'I truly mean you no harm, I am a friend of Harriet's and she sends you all her love.'

One by one they dropped the sticks and stones and moved closer to James.

'Why has Harriet not come to see us herself? She hasn't been to see us for a long time now', said Lily.

'Harriet is a very old lady now and she can't walk up here onto the moors any more, but she asked me to tell you that she misses you all very much', James assured them.

By now the situation had calmed right down and they were all relaxed. Some of them had even started to unwrap the sweets that James had laid out on the grass. James looked at these small childlike creatures and it was easy for him to understand how easily Harriet had fallen in love with them. Soon they were introducing themselves.

'I'm Alice, I'm Harry, I'm Gertrude, I'm Jack …' and so it went on.

'If Harriet can't come to us, then we'll go to her', stated Tommy.

'I don't think that's a very good idea, it would be far too dangerous for you', replied James.

'Well I'm still not sure that you are telling us the truth', said Tommy.

'Do you mean you still think Harriet is in the tape recorder box?' asked James.

'No, but I don't believe that she can't come up here to see us … can't you carry her? You're a big strong man', stated Tommy. All the others nodded in agreement.

'You know, there might just be a way I could bring Harriet up onto the moor. If I could drive her to the top of the hill in my car, would you be able to meet us near the gate at the top of the woods?' asked James.

'Yes, Yes', they all said. Then they began chanting again in their strange language. They got up and started to dance all around James, patting him on his head as they danced. James was overcome by the love he felt around him, he stood up and joined hands with them and danced along, joining in with the chanting, even though he had no idea what was being said.

This excitement amused James; he had certainly not expected to be dancing with the Trogglybogs. The most he had hoped for was to make contact with them.

'What would Harriet and Anna make of this?' he wondered to himself.

When the kerfuffle eventually calmed down, plans were discussed for how and when James would bring Harriet up onto the moors.

'I can drive my car up to the top of the lane as far as the edge of the moor, but I don't think Harriet will be able to walk very far, she is quite frail now', James told them.

'Don't worry about that, just you bring her to the top of the lane and we'll do the rest', said Tommy with a cheeky glint in his eye.

James wondered what he had in mind, but he didn't like to ask. He thought it would be best not to.

'When will you bring her to see us?' asked little Tosh. 'Will you bring her tomorrow?' asked another. The questions flew in thick and fast.

'I'll have to have a word with Harriet first, I don't know if she will agree to come.'

As soon as James had said that, he knew he had said the wrong thing; there were moans and some began to cry.

'No … no, don't worry! I'm sure she will, I'll talk her into it, it will be all right, but I just need to speak to her first before I can say when I will be able to bring her up here', said James, trying to reassure his newfound friends.

'You tell Harriet, if she won't come up here to see us then we'll come down to her. You will have to take us down to where Harriet lives', demanded Tommy.

Tommy could be very dominant for such a small person and James didn't want to get on the wrong side of him, so he just nodded his head in agreement. James also knew that if he told Harriet this she would have to agree to come with him onto the moors. Harriet had already expressed her fears for the Trogglybogs coming down to her cottage, so he knew that Tommy's threat would make it easier to talk her into agreeing to the plan.

James said he would speak to Harriet that same day and would come back up onto the moor that night at six o'clock, before it went dark, to let them know what she said.

Just as James was about to gather his things together, Tommy had a word of warning for him.

'James, whatever you do, you must tell no one about us. If you break that promise, you will never see any of us again.'

'Don't worry, I promise I won't breathe a word to anyone … but there's just one thing', said James. 'I assure you it's nothing to worry about, but my wife knows about you, and she knows that I've come up here to try to find you, but I promise you, she will not say a word to anyone … she's a good lady! And I trust her and so does Harriet.'

James waited with baited breath for Tommy's reaction; he knew that telling them this could destroy everything. He crossed his fingers and prayed that it wouldn't.

'Very well, we'll have to trust you, but not another soul must be told about us. Do you understand?' Tommy made it crystal clear and James knew there was no room for negotiation, not that he wanted to tell anyone else.

'I understand, and I promise you faithfully, no one else will be told. You have my word.' James held out his hand to Tommy and Tommy shook it. Everyone nodded their approval and James picked up his rucksack.

'Will you bring us some more sweets next time you come?' asked the one called Lily.

'I think I'm going to need my own sweets factory soon if I keep coming up here to see you!' said James. Everyone laughed and waved goodbye to him.

On his long walk back off the moor James had a wonderful smug feeling. He had achieved his goal – his plan with the tape-recorder had worked. Looking around he noticed that his foxy escort had joined him again. It was keeping a healthy distance, but following him.

Apart from the fox, James didn't see another living thing all the way off the moor. Even the birds that were usually fluttering around were nowhere to be seen. James stopped for a moment and just listened … The silence was deafening. Not a movement, no wind, no wildlife, no birds, no noise from the traffic could be heard. Just James and the fox! It all felt a bit eerie and yet very peaceful.

As he reached the gate at the top of the lane at the edge of the moor, James looked across at the fox. Again the fox appeared to nod its head up and down before it turned, running off in the direction it had come. James waved to the fox and smiled to himself, wondering what it was all about. Was it sent to see him off the moor by the Trogglybogs?

6

The Plan

James decided he would ask Tommy about the fox the next time he saw him. James's walk home, down the lane past the waterfall in the woods, was nothing more than a blur. When he finally reached the bottom of Well Lane, it suddenly occurred to him that he had been so deep in thought that he hadn't noticed any of his walk and yet here he was back in the village.

It was mid-afternoon by now and the village was quiet, apart from the odd car that was just passing through. It would be a lot different in an hour's time when the schools finished for the day. James tried to imagine what it would be like if all the village children suddenly disappeared, just as the children of the moors did 400 years ago. How their parents must have felt – they would have been frantic; it didn't bear thinking about!

As he arrived at the end of his road, James began to get very excited and couldn't wait to get into the house and tell Anna his news. He opened the door and was greeted with a wonderful smell of freshly baked cakes.

'Mmm, they smell good! I don't know whether to have one of them first or tell you my news', said James, with a cheeky and excited grin on his face.

'You're not going to tell me you found them are you? Because I won't believe you.'

'Well, yes I did find them, or should I say, they found me! And I have the cuts and bruises to prove it', said James, as he showed Anna his cut head and hands.

'Good heavens, what happened?'

Anna looked closely at James's head and told him to wait while she got some water and cotton wool. James laughed

'I'm all right honestly, don't fuss … it is well worth a few cuts and bruises to meet those creatures – sorry – children! I must stop calling them creatures. They truly are wonderful, and I've told them that you know about them, so maybe you can come and meet them yourself soon.'

'No thank you, not if that's how they treat their friends', said Anna, laughing.

James told Anna everything that had happened, how the Trogglybogs had thought Harriet was inside the tape-recorder and about the fox following him off the moor again.

'We need to go and see Harriet. I have to try to get her to agree to come to the top of the lane. Do you think she will?' asked James.

'After what you've told me I'm sure she will. Just let me take this last tray of cakes out of the oven, and I'll come down to her house with you.'

Anna put some cakes in a bag for Harriet and they set off. James took the dogs with him; he knew that might be the only walk they would get that day if he was going to go back onto the moors to see the Trogglybogs after tea.

Arriving at Harriet's cottage, James tied up the two dogs. Harriet was round the side of the house doing a bit of tidying up and pruning her bushes.

'Hello there, they get so long you know and I can't get down the path' said Harriet, indicating towards the blackthorn and the raspberry bushes.

Harriet had quite a large garden for such a small cottage; much of it was overgrown and unmanageable.

'I have a young man who comes round in the summer months and keeps it tidy for me, I used to enjoy doing it myself when I was younger, but it's too much for me now.'

'Harriet, I have some wonderful news for you', said James.

'Did your plan work?' enquired Harriet in an incredulous tone.

'It most certainly did, let's go inside and I'll tell you all about my day.'

'Before you begin, I'll make some tea and we can have one of Anna's cakes.'

Harriet would not be rushed; it was always tea first, before any discussion. This amused James and Anna, but they didn't mind, Harriet was a lovely lady; Anna had suggested to James that she did this in order to keep them there a little longer, just for the company.

Once the ritual of the tea was out of the way, James told Harriet what had happened that day. Harriet burst out laughing.

'Oh I'm sorry, I shouldn't laugh, but I can understand them believing that I was inside the tape machine. They will never have seen anything like that gadget before – I mean, just put yourself in their shoes – 400 years on the moors and they have never seen anything, not even a radio or a television. I have told them about televisions and things like that, but they used to look at me like I was mad', said Harriet.

James took a deep breath and told Harriet about the plan that Tommy and him had for taking her up onto the moors.

'I can drive you right up Well Lane as far as the gate at the top of the hill, from there it is only a few feet and you're on the moor itself. Tommy and the others will meet us there if you agree to it.' James waited, looking at the fear and apprehension on Harriet's face; he feared the worst.

'Tommy says if you don't go and see him, he will come here to see you … and I think he means it too!' said James, hoping that this would help her to agree.

'But I haven't been further than the village store for twenty years or more. My legs are very weak nowadays and the paths onto the moor are so rough and stony.'

'Don't worry, I'll be with you every inch of the way, I won't let any harm come to you and it is only a few feet, you can even wait in the car until I make sure they're there to meet us. It's either that or Tommy will come here to your cottage – he's adamant about seeing you again!'

'You can trust James', said Anna. 'He won't let you come to any harm.'

'Very well then', said Harriet. 'When are we going?' Now Harriet seemed to be rather excited. James gave a big sigh of relief.

'I told Tommy that if you agreed, I would go back to see him tonight and make the arrangements. We can go any day this week, any day you like!' said James. After some thought, they decided Friday was best. It would give Harriet a little time to get used to the idea. James jumped up and took hold of Harriet's hand.

'You won't be sorry; it will be so exciting for you to see all your little friends again. If I'm to make it up onto the moors before it goes dark I'd better get my skates on'.

'C'mon Anna, let's be making tracks. It's half past five now; it'll be dark soon enough.'

James was up and halfway through the door before Anna had even put her coat on.

'Goodnight Harriet, I'll call round tomorrow to tell you what they said.' James gave Harriet a quick wave and he was off down the garden path with the two dogs. Anna gave Harriet a kiss, and a look that questioned James's sanity.

'You'll have to excuse him, when he makes up his mind to do something, wild horses won't stop him … he's just excited!'

'I know how he feels. I'm beginning to get rather excited too!' said Harriet.

Anna called after James.

'James, I've got an idea, why don't you go down under the bridge and up through the woods onto the moors? I can take the dogs home. It will save you a lot of time.'

'Are you sure you will be all right going home by yourself?' asked James 'It certainly would save me a lot of time if I did that.'

'Of course I'll be all right, nobody is going to bother me with these two dogs by my side.'

James laughed, he knew that Bracken certainly wouldn't let anyone harm Anna, but Skip was just the opposite, he was a right old softie – certainly no guard dog!

With that James pushed on past the Hall, down under the bridge and into the woods. The light was already beginning to fade, but it didn't bother James, he knew those woods and moors like the back of his hand. Soon James was at the waterfall, from which there were two paths that James could take to the top of the moors, he could walk round the main path and follow the road, or he could take the short cut and go further up through the wood.

James decided that because it was already beginning to get dark he would take the quick route through the woods. The path from there was no more than a single track, made by walkers who took their dogs that way. James had himself often taken his dogs along there. That path went all the way round the outer perimeter of the wood, but James only had to walk the first five hundred yards or so to the top of the moor. It was very densely overgrown and along the way there was the odd broken-down ruin of cottages that had been inhabited over a hundred years ago. All that was visible of these ruins now were piles of stone but it was possible to make out the shapes of where the walls had been. James had often wondered when he had passed them what it must have been like living up there in the woods all those years ago. Life would have been much slower then … not the hustle and bustle that we know today. No computers, not even aeroplanes or cars were around then!

James arrived at the top of the wood and at that point there was a stile over the wall leading onto the moor itself. As James approached the stile he was met by his friend the fox. James stopped in his tracks, looked at the fox and the fox looked back at him. James moved to take a step forward towards the stile, and as he did the fox moved slowly to the side as if allowing him access to the stile. James took another step forward, watching the fox all the time. The fox continued to move to the side, but didn't run off as you would imagine a wild animal would do. This was strange; he had never known anything like this before – it had to be something to do with the Trogglybogs!

Nervously, James reached the stile and with one eye on the fox he put his first foot onto the stile. As he did the fox began to nod its head as it had done before. It seemed to be a sign of approval, as if to say 'OK, you've reached your destination.'

Then suddenly and with such noise, out of the grass jumped the Trogglybogs, they were all around him, some only inches away.

'Where on earth did you lot come from? I didn't see you sneaking up on me, I was too busy watching that fox!' gasped James.

Even the fox was jumping up and down and joining in the excitement.

'I knew that fox was something to do with you lot, he's

followed me a few times when I've been coming off the moor …
he's been like an escort!'

'That's right', said Tommy. 'That was the idea, but don't
worry he's a good friend of ours … his name is Harry!'

Harry the fox walked up to James, sat down and offered his
paw to shake. James was amazed.

'This is unbelievable. How do you do Harry?' asked James.
Harry nodded his head again and everyone laughed.

'Right, did you speak with Harriet?' asked Tommy.

'Yes, and its good news … she will come up here with me on
Friday. I am going to drive her to the top of the lane as far as I
can and then I will have to help her the rest of the way, so it
would be good if you could meet us as close as possible to the
gate'. Everyone cheered at James's good news.

'Don't you worry about that, just you bring her as far as the
gate and we'll do the rest', declared Tommy.

'I think it might be best if we come up here as early as possible
on Friday morning; I thought about six o'clock if that's not too
early!' said James. 'At least there shouldn't be anyone knocking
about at that time in the morning.'

'That's fine', said Tommy and all the others agreed.

'So six o'clock in the morning on Friday it is', agreed James.

'Well, this has been a memorable day, it's so wonderful to
have met you all, and Harriet's just as excited as you about
Friday … I don't think I'll be able to sleep tonight, with all this
excitement.'

James was over the moon at having found the Trogglybogs
of Brinscall Moor. He felt like telling the world, but he knew it
would be the end if he were to tell anyone; they had to remain
a secret. James wished them all a goodnight and set off down
the hill towards the village.

By now it was getting quite dark and the woods at night
were pretty spooky, but James was so happy at having had
such an exciting day that nothing was going to scare him
tonight.

James arrived home just as Anna was putting the finishing

touches to the evening meal.

'That's the second time I've walked in to the smell of something good today', James said.

'Your timing is good, I'll give you that. How did you go on? Did you see them?' asked Anna.

'I certainly did and they were over the moon at the news that Harriet has agreed to meet them. I was also right about that fox! He was there again, he is a friend of the Trogglybogs, his name is Harry and I've even shaken paws with him', said James.

'You've shaken hands with a fox! This gets more bizarre every time you go out. I think you need to see a doctor!' Anna laughed, 'I'm going to have to meet these Trogglybogs, they sound too good to be true.'

'Next time I see them I'll ask them if they will agree to see you, if you want.'

James and Anna sat down to their meal and James told Anna the full story about his latest encounter with the fox.

7

The Reunion

Thursday evening came and James decided he would go down to Harriet's, just to make sure she was all right, and ready for an early morning start tomorrow.

James knocked at the door and waited for the usual sound of all the bolts coming off. Surely enough, one by one the bolts clunked open and the door opened to reveal Harriet's frail frame. 'She must only weigh six stone', James thought to himself. Five feet tall, six stone, and living in the middle of nowhere all by herself. Her green eyes sparkled as she saw James.

'Come in, come in ... I'm so excited about tomorrow; you've not come to tell me we're not going, have you?' Harriet's face dropped.

Good heavens, no! I've just come to make sure you are still OK for an early morning start, that's all', said James reassuringly.

'Oh good, of course I'm all right ... I'd go now if you wanted to, I can't wait. I just hope my legs will hold out.'

'Don't you worry. Tommy and the others are going to meet us as soon as the car stops and anyway, I would carry you if I had to', laughed James.

'Would you like some tea?' asked Harriet.

'No thanks, this is just a quick visit, I must be on my way – I have things to do. I'll see you at about five thirty in the morning ... Goodnight!'

James left Harriet's and as he was walking out of the gate he met PC Hoyle.

'Now then James, what are you doing round here? I didn't know you knew Miss Bond.'

'Good evening, Constable. I just call in now and again to make sure the old lady is OK. Harriet is more a friend of Anna's really', said James.

'That's good of you James, it's quite lonely down here at the best of times, so it's good to see people are looking out for one another'. PC Hoyle smiled, tipped his hat and went on his way.

'I hope he's not on his rounds at half five in the morning', thought James 'How would we explain that?'

Walking back up the lane James's eyes looked over towards the moors, and he couldn't help wondering if the Trogglybogs were as excited about tomorrow as he and Harriet were. When he reached the shop James tied the dogs to the railings and went inside.

'I can't go up there emptyhanded', he thought. He picked up a basket and proceeded to fill it with sweets. He was pleased to see that Peggy wasn't on the counter that night; she had given him enough earache the last time he bought sweets by the basketful. No doubt Anna would tell him off, but at least she knew the real reason why he's buying them; so he wouldn't have to explain too much to her.

'£10.68 please', said the lady behind the counter, thankfully not enquiring as to why he wanted so many sweets.

James paid, picked up his bag, collected the dogs and went home. Anna took one look at the bag, shook her head but said nothing.

'I think I'll have a cup of tea, a bath and an early night. I've got an early start in the morning', said James.

'Just as long as you don't wake me', replied Anna.

The clock went off at exactly five o'clock; James reached out and switched the alarm off almost as soon as it started to ring. He turned to look at Anna, but she was still fast asleep. James had a quick shower, went downstairs and made himself a cup of tea and some toast. It was now twenty past five. James knew it would only take him a minute or two to drive down to Harriet's. It was a good fifteen minutes walking but he was not walking this morning. He collected his bag of sweets and he even took a handful of the dogs' biscuits, just in case Harry was there.

The road down past the Hall was rough, with large boulders sticking up in places. James had to be very careful; if he hit one of these large stones it might rip the bottom of his car clean off. Once down at the bottom where Harriet lived there was plenty of room to turn the car around and park. Before he had the chance to get out of the car, Harriet was out of the house and halfway down the garden path.

It was now almost daylight and Harriet was wrapped up in a warm coat and hat; although it was late April it was still quite cold first thing.

'Good morning Harriet, you are keen', laughed James as he opened the car door for her.

'I've hardly slept a wink, I'm so excited', said Harriet.

James helped the frail old lady into the car and fastened her seat belt for her.

'I've not been in a car for years, the last time was when I had to go to hospital and they sent a taxi cab for me. That must be over thirty years ago now', said Harriet.

James smiled, started the engine and off they went up the bumpy road.

'This road wasn't made for cars and that's for sure', said James, as he avoided the rocks and potholes.

'No it was all right for the horses and carts, but it has got a lot worse over the years since the railway shut down', said Harriet.

As soon as James reached the Hall he was able to go much faster. The road from the Hall was a well-made road of tarmac, long and straight with big trees lining both sides all the way up to the village. James arrived at the main road and turned right down the village. Harriet could see the moors across the valley. Her heart began to race with excitement; she knew that in a few moments she would be meeting her beloved little friends once again.

'James, I can't thank you enough for doing this for me, I have missed them so much.' A tear ran down Harriet's cheek and James offered her a tissue from the box he kept on the dashboard.

'I hope those are tears of happiness', said James, who was also beginning to get a little emotional.

Harriet laughed and blew her nose. 'I'll be all right now', she said.

The car reached the bottom of the village and went over the main road and up the lane, through the woods, past the waterfall and into open space. This was the last few hundred yards to the top of the moors. In a matter of seconds they had arrived at the very top and the car could go no further. James pulled up to the left of the gate and then reversed – parking well out of the way of any other vehicles that might have to come up onto the moors, such as the farmer's Land Rover or tractor.

James switched off the engine, got out of the car and walked round to help Harriet out. He opened the door and taking her hand, he helped her to her feet.

'I hope they turn up', said James, his eyes looking all around for any signs.

'Don't you worry, they're here! I just know it', replied Harriet.

James helped Harriet the twenty or so feet to the gate and once through she stopped to catch her breath. This was very harsh terrain even for the experienced walkers that came up here. It certainly was not the place for a little old lady who was bad on her legs.

Harriet was just about to sit down on the edge of the stile when there was the biggest cheer you have ever heard. All twenty-four of the Trogglybogs had come to meet Harriet and the noise was deafening. Cheering, whistling, shouting and singing, everyone was running around throwing lumps of grass into the air.

'She's here! She's here! Hurrah for Harriet!'

Then Tommy let out a very loud shrill whistle and everyone stopped.

'Harriet, it is so good to see you again, but how you've changed ... so old! I remember my parents and grandparents looking old like you ... if only! If only!' repeated Tommy.

'Oh never mind that. Do I not get a hug?' asked Harriet. And with that they were all around her, hugging and kissing her and holding her hand.

'Harriet, you must spend the day with us at least', said Tommy. 'You can stay forever if you want!' stated Lilybog.

Harriet laughed, 'Well at my age that won't be for very long.' Everyone began to laugh, and then Tommy said, 'But that's what I meant when I said – if only. When my parents were old I could do nothing for them, but now we have the power ... the power that we got from the Saxons ... and now, anything is possible!'

'James, stand back over there, I promise no harm will come to you or Harriet, but I must show you what I mean.'

'Harriet, I'm not so sure I like this', said a very worried James.

'Don't worry, I know my friends won't hurt us ... Just do as they ask, everything will be all right', Harriet assured James.

As James moved away all the Trogglybogs gathered round Harriet, forming two circles. They began to nod their heads, then one circle danced round Harriet one way and the other circle moved in the opposite direction. As they did, Tommy took out something from a pouch and threw it into the air above Harriet. It was like a sparkling silver dust and it glittered in the early morning sunlight. Then they all began to chant and the dancing became faster and faster until it was a blur. It was soon so frantic and going at such a speed that it resembled a tornado, dust flew up from the ground and spiralled skywards. The noise and the wind forced James to move even further away, until he could not see anything of Harriet among all the dust and he was worried for her safety. This went on for no more than a half a minute, then it stopped suddenly and all was calm.

James lifted his head and looking towards the circles, he tried to see if Harriet was OK, but there was no sign of her. He ran towards the Trogglybogs and as he did, out of the middle of the frenzy stepped a small girl, aged about ten.

'Harriet, Harriet, is that you?' enquired James.

'Yes it's me, isn't it wonderful?' beamed Harriet.

'You can remain like that as long as you stay on the moor with us,' said Tommy, 'but if you choose to leave the moor, you will go back to being your old-aged self again.'

James was astounded. Harriet had told him that they had magic powers, but this was just unbelievable; they had turned Harriet back to the age she was when they first met her.

It was now almost seven o'clock and there was a chance that early morning walkers would begin to come onto the moors soon. Tommy suggested they move off.

'James,' he said, 'how would you like to come to see our caves? We've prepared some food for you and we'd like you and Harriet to be our guests If you would do us the honour!'

James thanked Tommy; the prospect of going down into the caverns thrilled him.

'We have another surprise for you James, take hold of our hands and hold tight.'

As he did, his feet lifted off the ground and he was flying fast over the moors. The ground whizzed by beneath him at incredible speed, up over the hills and down the valleys they soared, up over the top of Great Hill and down the gully towards White Coppice, eventually stopping at the foot of the gully. It was a part of the gully known to James as 'Devil's Valley', just a nickname that James and some of his fellow walkers had given it because of its huge size.

Harriet said 'Oh, I remember this place, but it's the first time I've ever flown here, that was wonderful.'

James was shaking; he had not imagined when he got up that morning that he would have seen or done anything like this. Anna would never believe it.

'Right now you two, keep hold of our hands, and James, you can close your eyes if you want to', laughed Tommy.

8

The Labyrinth

James looked at Harriet; the smile on her face suggested there was nothing to worry about. Tosh was soon alongside James, as was Lily; they took hold of James's hands and told him not to worry.

'You're going to love this', Harriet said excitedly. 'The caverns are amazing.'

As they walked towards a big rock that was embedded in the hillside, James tried hard to keep his eyes open, but the moment he got there, he felt like he was going to walk straight into the solid face and try as he might his eyes shut tight in anticipation of the immediate impact.

'It's all right James, you can open your eyes now', laughed Lily.

James opened his eyes to find himself inside a well-lit tunnel, it wasn't very high, but when he thought about it, the Trogglybogs didn't need much height.

'You might need to bend down in some places James; you'll be all right once we reach the caverns – it's very high in there', said Tommy.

Off they all went: the tunnel was like a flight of stairs at first and then it levelled out. It began to bend left and then right and there were side tunnels branching off in all directions. All the tunnels were very well-lit with torches; it reminded James of a medieval castle. After walking for two or three minutes, the party turned sharp right into a huge cavern. It was like an underground world with a massive lagoon and the land that

surrounded it was sandy and beach-like. The roof of the cavern had large stones embedded in it, that shone like brightly coloured diamonds, lighting up the whole cavern.

The lake was teeming with fish that playfully jumped out of the water. The fish were all sizes and beautifully coloured. At the far end of the cavern, a waterfall cascaded down from the roof, over rocks and into the lagoon: it made a wonderful noise – tranquil and calming. It was also quite warm, and not in the least bit damp, as you might imagine it would be.

Tommy led the party round the lake to an area that had been prepared for the day's festivities. Tables were laid and seats set out. Unfortunately, the seating that the Trogglybogs had was not designed for someone of James's size.

'Oh dear, we hadn't thought of that', Tommy said, somewhat embarrassed by the oversight. 'No matter!' He called four of his companions over and soon they were running off down a passageway. A couple of minutes later they re-emerged carrying what appeared to be a large wooden throne.

'Where on earth did you get that from? asked James.

'That, James, belonged to the leader of the Saxons and he gave us permission to use it for very special guests only. The last person to sit on that throne was a man called King Charles, but that was a long time ago, in 1648 I think! We hid him from some bad men who were trying to kill him. I should imagine he will be dead now anyway, it being such a long time since!' said Tommy.

'Yes Tommy, he most certainly is dead', assured James.

'Oh, so you knew him did you?' enquired Tommy.

'Good heavens, no! But I have read about him in history books.'

'Did the books mention us?' asked Lily.

'No, I imagine the King wanted to keep your secret safe – just like we do!'

As James sat down on the mighty Saxon throne, and placed his arms on the armrests, he lost himself in his thoughts for a moment.

'To think … King Charles I sat in this very same seat, just over three hundred years before, and no one has sat in it since.' James felt very honoured. Harriet and the Trogglybogs looked at James approvingly.

'You look just right for that seat – just like a king!' said Harriet.

'Yes, except your hair isn't as long as King Charles!' stated little Tosh.

Everyone burst out laughing. Tosh was the smallest of all the Trogglybogs; all the others were about two feet tall, but Tosh was only about eighteen inches and had a slightly squeaky voice to go with her size. Everyone thought she was funny and seemed to laugh at everything she said, but this didn't bother her, it just made her do things more; she loved the attention.

'After we've eaten, we'll take you on a grand tour of our underground world and we'll show you the magic cavern that is the Saxons' resting place', Tommy said.

'My, you are honoured, James', declared Harriet. 'I've been

down these caves a few times before, but I've not been taken to the Saxon cavern!'

'Well, I feel we owe James a great debt for bringing you back to us, so this is a special treat for everyone', said Tommy.

Everyone cheered, and then the food began to arrive. James couldn't help noticing that everything was vegetarian. It had been prepared beautifully and looked delicious. There were pancakes, bread, cheese and all different kinds of what appeared to be mushrooms; there was lots of fresh fruit and vegetables, there were pots and pots of jam of all flavours.

'Yes James, it is all vegetarian!' declared Tommy.

'Did you know I was thinking that? Or do your guests usually ask?'

'I knew you were thinking there's no meat on the table, the reason is that we don't eat meat. All the animals are our friends and we don't eat our friends.'

'I can agree with that, and anyway the food looks and smells wonderful', said James.

Before dining Tommy asked everyone to be silent for a moment, to remember friends and family who could no longer join them and enjoy the feast. After saying grace, the party got under way. Everyone passed the various dishes round the large table, making sure that Harriet and James were first to be offered the food. James couldn't help but think what good manners they had.

Within an hour almost all the food had gone, the Trogglybogs had repeatedly filled up their guests' plates time and again. James felt like he was about to burst and Harriet wasn't much better.

'Tommy – all of you, that was delicious. Thank you all so much!' James said.

'Likewise', said Harriet.

'Shall we play some games now?' asked Tosh.

'I don't think I could', said James.

'No, much better to walk off a good meal', declared Tommy. 'We can go for that tour of the caverns if you like, James?'

'I think that might be a better idea. No offence, Tosh, but I'm full to bursting', said James.

'Me too', declared Harriet.

This created more laughter. They seemed to laugh at just about anything and everything, their sense of humour was wonderful.

On this decision everyone stood up and began to collect all the plates and trays together, they then took them down to the edge of the lagoon and just threw them all in. James looked on in disbelief as all the wooden dishes and plates were thrown into the water.

'Don't worry,' said Harriet, 'the fish will do the washing-up.'

James looked at her and he could tell she was serious. 'This just gets more bizarre', he thought to himself.

'I told you James, all the animals are our friends, and that includes the fish', chuckled Tommy. 'When we come back, all the dishes will have been washed and will be stacked up on the shore for us.'

All the Trogglybogs stood looking at James and nodding.

'Amazing … truly amazing', said James in disbelief.

'Follow me', said Tommy. And off he strode. 'You will have to keep up and mind you don't get lost James, these tunnels are a labyrinth of passageways, they branch off in all directions and you could be wandering around lost for ages. I think we'll show you the Saxons' cavern first, and we can give them thanks for the magic powers they gave us that enabled us to bring Harriet here today', said Tommy.

'This is very exciting. Are you all right, Harriet?' asked James.

'I'm fine.' Harriet took hold of James's hand and gave it a squeeze. Tosh was quick to take hold of his other hand; she had quite clearly taken a shine to James.

The walk to the Saxon cave was quite a long way, but James didn't mind: the thought of entering this place of magic thrilled him, although it also made him a little nervous. After all, some of the things he had read about the Saxons had portrayed them as fierce warriors. He recalled the history books about Boadicea and how she had slain 75,000 Romans, but he had the Trogglybogs on his side, so he should be all right, he hoped!

The walk took them on an uphill climb for about two hundred yards and then down a steep winding path and in some places the tunnel was barely wide or high enough for James to get through, but he was getting reassurances all the way from his newfound friends. Everywhere they went and every tunnel they entered, the stones seemed to light up as they entered it, making it bright.

'I wish I had this kind of lighting at home', James said to Harriet. Harriet laughed. 'I'll show you something when we get back', she said.

James looked at her. Surely she couldn't have this lighting in her house – could that be what she meant? He didn't question her about it then, he was doing all he could not to bang his head on the low roof of the tunnel.

One final right turn and they had arrived in the cavern that was beneath the Saxon burial grounds. This cavern wasn't as big as the one where the Trogglybogs lived and there was no lagoon, but right in the centre of the cave was a huge rock and laid out around it were the swords, shields and various items of pottery, placed there by the Trogglybogs.

'Those things were all around here when we first found this cavern, and some were still hanging down from the roof of the cave', said Tommy. 'We knew they must have been special and when we found some bones we realized they must have fallen from a grave above, so we thought it would be the proper thing to do, to re-bury them and after we did the spirit of the Saxon chief spoke to us and thanked us. He told us we would be well looked after and that we would develop magic powers – and we did!'

Tommy and the rest of the Trogglybogs walked over to the rock and knelt down, and began to give thanks to the Saxons for the magic they had been given, and for making it possible, through that magic, to be able to bring Harriet onto the moors again.

All was quiet and very peaceful. Tommy then stood up and passed James one of the swords that was laying on top of the grave that was the Saxon chief's. It was made of silver and was very heavy.

'Those Saxons must have been very strong to have been able to fight with these', said James.

Then James spotted on the side of the big rock, something that looked like prehistoric cave paintings.

'Did you paint these?' he asked Tommy.

'No, they were there long before we found this cave. It might have been the Saxons though!' replied Tommy.

James looked at them closely and knew that these caves had probably been inhabited long before the Saxons had walked these hills. James placed the sword back down on the ground exactly where Tommy had picked it up from. He looked up towards the roof of the cave; it was easy to see why Tommy and the others had believed these things had fallen from graves above. James could just make out more bones sticking through.

'It looks like more bones will drop down here soon' he said, pointing up to the roof.

'Well, when they do we will bury them along with the others', declared Tommy. 'I don't think we could have survived as long as this if we hadn't had the help of the spirits, so we must look after them in return.'

Before leaving, all the Trogglybogs faced the big rock and bowed, then they said 'thank you'.

Once outside the Saxon cave the mood became less sombre. Little Tosh and Lily ran on ahead laughing and whispering amongst themselves.

'What are you two up to?' asked Tommy.

'Let's show James and Harriet the new cavern that we've found … the one with the black pond', said Lily

'Yes, it's very scary in there', agreed Tosh.

'What's this about a new cavern?' asked Harriet. 'Is it one you've found since I was last here?'

'Yes, but I don't think you would like it in there, it is dark and the pond in there has no fish in it. The water is as black as the night. It's quite a big cave, but very spooky, we don't go in there much', said Tommy.

'Oh go on, let's have a look in', pleaded Tosh.

Harriet agreed, 'Yes I'd like to see the new cave, I've seen all the others.'

'Very well', said Tommy, and off they all went.

'It's right at the far end, deep under the brown hill', said Tommy. To get to it they had to walk for ages deep down underground for half a mile. By the time they reached the brown hill the lights that were embedded in the walls of the cave were far and few between. Tommy and some of the others lit torches to make it brighter.

'Here we are then; just down here ... mind your head, James!' warned Tommy.

The entrance to the new cave was only four feet high and James had to bend right down. The Trogglybogs had no such problem and even Harriet made it without having to bend too much.

Once inside, it was obvious that this cavern wasn't like any of the others they had visited that day. It was large, very cold and damp. The pond in the middle of the cave was very still, unlike the main cavern which was teeming with fish that jumped up out of the water all the time. This water was stagnant and as black as oil.

James looked around the walls to see if he could see any more of the cave paintings he had seen in the Saxon cavern, but there were none to be found. Tommy joined James as he walked around.

'What is so important about the paintings you found? Do you think the Saxons painted them?' asked Tommy.

'No, not the Saxons, but people who lived on these moors long before them, you see, many years ago people used to live in caves ...'

Then suddenly, as James was explaining to Tommy what he

meant, there was a deafening scream.

James spun round to see Harriet scrambling away from the water's edge. Her feet slipped into the water as she desperately tried to climb the banking, and in the confusion, Lily who had been with her, suddenly slipped and fell into the pond. James dashed over, slid down the bank, grabbed Lily and pulled her out of the cold black slimy water.

Harriet was crying and shaking. Lily didn't appear to be too bad for her part of the ordeal.

'Harriet, are you all right?' Tommy asked as he rushed over to where the two frightened and wet girls were. 'What happened, did you slip into the pond?'

'I did,' said Lily, 'and it's jolly cold in there. I can tell you.'

Harriet was trembling and crying; she pointed over to the water, but couldn't speak for sobbing. Everyone huddled round the two of them, hugging and reassuring them.

'Harriet, what happened? What's frightened you so much? Did you think you were going to fall in?' asked James. By now Harriet was beginning to calm down.

'In the water over there … when I looked into the water I saw a face – it was horrible!' she began to cry again.

'It was just your reflection in the oily black water. You probably just looked a little distorted in this bad light', said James, trying to calm her down.

'No – I know what I saw and it certainly wasn't my reflection. It was an evil face! Please, take me out of here.' She got up and ran towards the entrance of the cavern, quickly followed by Lily, followed by everyone else.

'Did you see the face in the water?' Tommy asked Lily.

'No, I just fell in because Harriet startled me', replied Lily.

This made everyone laugh – everyone except Harriet that is. Tommy and James hugged Harriet as they made their way back along the half-mile tunnel. The further away from the black cavern they got, the lighter and warmer it became. By the time they had reached the main cavern, both girls were dry; Harriet had stopped shaking and had dried her tears. Tommy ordered hot drinks all round to cheer everyone up.

'I know what I saw in there: it was the face of a very old woman and she had hatred in her eyes. You must block up that cave and never go in there again. Promise me!' pleaded Harriet to Tommy.

'Well, we don't like going down there anyway. I'll take some of the others and we'll block it off tomorrow', promised Tommy.

Harriet gave a big sigh of relief at hearing Tommy say that. James looked at his watch and announced it was time they should be leaving. This brought sighs and moans from all quarters, along with an upsetting reminder from Tommy.

'Remember what I said when you came onto the moor Harriet, if you decide to leave the moors – you will go back to being an old woman again!'. Harriet looked at Tommy and all the other Trogglybogs, and smiled.

'I know, but I am still the same Harriet that came onto the moors, and although you've changed me back to how I used to be years ago, I have to go back to myself, to how I should be. I'm too old and too tired to be starting life all over again. I've had my time and it's been wonderful to come up here and see you all again, but I must go back to my home. Who knows? Maybe James will bring me again one day.'

Although Harriet was smiling, she was also crying. It had been a wonderful experience for her, seeing all her little friends again after more than twenty years and she knew it might be the last time she would ever see them. She realized that, being over eighty years old, the chances of her being able to keep coming onto the moors were getting less and less. It was only thanks to James's kindness that it had been possible this time.

'We can come and see you', said Tommy.

'No. I absolutely forbid it!' said Harriet. 'It is far too dangerous for you to leave the moors. If you were to be seen, you would be hunted down like wild animals. You must never try to come to my house.'

'I will bring Harriet back here again to see you. We'll have to arrange another time, but Harriet's right … it will be too dangerous for you down in the village', said James.

'Very well', agreed Tommy reluctantly.

As they made their way up the steps and into the passage that led outside and back onto the moors, they all linked hands and walked out through the rock. James again closed his eyes. The thought of walking into solid rock seemed impossible and no matter how he tried, he couldn't imagine not hurting himself.

James knew immediately that he was outside; he could feel the wind on his face.

'Are we flying back?' he asked.

'No', said Tommy. 'We're walking. I want us to enjoy every last moment with Harriet that we can and if we walk, that will give us a little longer.' Tommy laughed.

As they walked back off the moor, they were again joined by Harry the fox, only this time he walked along with them instead of at a distance. Walking along the path towards where James had left his car, James spotted, in the distance, a group of people approaching.

'Quickly – hide!' he instructed the Trogglybogs.

'Don't worry,' said Tommy, 'they won't know we're here.'

As the people got closer and closer, James got more and more anxious. The Trogglybogs just carried on walking. Soon the people had met with James and Harriet. James looked down and surely enough the Trogglybogs were still walking along side them.

'Good afternoon', the group of people said one by one to James and Harriet.

'Hmmm, good afternoon', said James, nervously.

James looked down and his companions were still alongside him and smiling. Then it dawned on James: the Trogglybogs were invisible to those people! When they were a safe enough distance not to be heard, James asked, 'How come we can see you and they didn't?'

Tommy just tapped the side of his nose and winked at James. It was more Trogglybog magic. James laughed; he had never had so much fun. Then it suddenly occurred to him – if they could make themselves invisible to those people, why could they not visit Harriet at her cottage? Tommy explained to James.

'It would be wonderful if it were as simple as that, but unfortunately, our magic only works as long as we remain on the moors; once we leave them, our power weakens and we might be seen.'

As they all arrived at the gate where James had parked his car, the mood became sad again. They knew that their dear friend Harriet was leaving and they feared they might not see her again for a long time, and maybe never again! Harriet hugged and kissed every one of them, and with tears running down her cheeks she promised them she would come back soon.

James opened the car doors and Harriet and himself got in. They gave one last wave and James drove off. He had not driven more than a few yards when he noticed that the little girl he had spent all day with had turned back into the frail old lady he had taken onto the moors earlier that day.

He stopped the car.

'Are you sure this is what you want?' he asked her.

'Yes, it has to be', replied Harriet.

James had had a wonderful day, but seeing Harriet as an old woman again saddened him. The only good thing was that he knew it could all be done again, and next time Harriet might decide to remain as a small girl. It seemed such a waste to have her as an old woman, when only a few moments ago, she was a lively young girl.

9

Anna's Meeting

As James drove down the lane and past the Hall, grey squirrels were busy foraging for scraps of food, and a roe deer was grazing in the field beyond Harriet's cottage. Hares were playing in the afternoon sun. Seeing all this going on made James realize why anyone would want to live where Harriet lived. This was nature at its best, and James was beginning to envy Harriet.

'I often wondered why anyone would want to live down here, so far away from anywhere, but seeing all these animals makes me think you're very lucky'.

James pulled up and walked round to help Harriet out of the car. It took almost as long to reach her front door as it did to make the drive from the top of the moors.

'Will you come in for a cup of tea?' asked Harriet.

James couldn't refuse. 'I would love one', he said.

Although he had only known Harriet for a short while, James had become very fond of her. Strange really, because he knew nothing about her, except that she was a lovely old lady. Harriet came in with the tea tray and some biscuits.

'How long have you lived here?' James asked her.

'All my life. Or as long as I can remember! I lived here with my mother up until I was fifteen and then she went away to visit a sick relative. She died suddenly while she was away. I was notified by letter. I didn't even get to go to the funeral. It was all done with by the time the letter reached me.'

'What about your father?' asked James.

'I never knew him and mother would not speak about him – to this day, I don't know who he was.'

Harriet smiled, 'It doesn't bother me. After I left school I took up nursing and I was a district nurse for nearly all my working life. I threw myself into my work and when I wasn't working I spent my time with my little friends up on the moors.'

'Have you never been married?' James asked her.

Harriet laughed. 'Good heavens, no – I've had no time for that – far too busy!'

'Now then, before I forget. I promised to show you something.' Harriet went into her bedroom and came back with a table lamp.

'Look at that', she instructed James.

James took the lamp and began to examine it. Under the shade, instead of a bulb there was a piece of white rock fitted into where the bulb should have been.

'Just touch the stone', said Harriet.

James did, and the stone lit up as bright as any lamp. 'That's amazing', he chuckled to himself.

'Tommy gave me that stone over fifty years ago and it is still as good as the day he gave it to me. I fitted it into that lamp a few years ago, and I keep it at my bedside. It's wonderful considering I don't have any electricity down here. All my other lights are gas.'

'Why have you never had electricity put in?' James enquired.

'Just never got around to it. And I'm too old to bother now', said Harriet.

James kept touching the stone, switching it on and off.

'When anything happens to me, you can have that lamp, but until then I need it for my bedside. Harriet could see how the stone in the lamp fascinated James, but then again, it would fascinate anyone: it was the only one of its kind in the world.

James finished his tea and gave the lamp back to Harriet.

'Thank you, I hope I won't become its owner for a very long time yet … and remember, if you were to take up Tommy's offer and stay with them on the moor …' Harriet stopped him in his tracks.

'No, I don't want that kind of life – the thought of living forever might appeal to some folk, but not me! So let's not talk about that again ... all right?' Harriet was adamant.

'OK, I promise not to mention it again', he said.

Harriet smiled. 'More tea?'

'No thanks, I'd better be going. I told Anna I wouldn't be too long. That was over eight hours ago', said James, looking at his watch.

'Will you be all right?' he asked Harriet. 'It's been rather an exciting day for you; it's been an exciting day for all of us, come to think of it!'

'I'll be fine. I haven't had so much fun in years', chuckled Harriet.

James picked up his coat, gave Harriet a kiss and made his way to the door. Harriet waved him off as he made his way down the path. He'd had the most amazing day of his life and he couldn't wait to tell Anna all about it. As his car pulled up at the door, Anna opened the front door and the two dogs bounced out to greet him.

'I thought you weren't going to be long, I've been worried', said Anna.

She was clearly upset and somewhat angry.

'I'm sorry, but when I tell you what has happened, you won't believe it'.

'I think you had better take these dogs out for a walk before you do anything', snapped Anna.

James could see that taking the dogs out was probably the best thing to do, otherwise he might end up in the doghouse himself. Anna needed time to calm down. It was his own fault though; he had been gone for far longer than he had led Anna to believe. By the time he had returned from his walk, Anna was much calmer and had James's tea ready for him.

'I'm sorry I was out for so long, but I have had the most unbelievable day. You must come up onto the moors and meet the Trogglybogs ... they have to be seen to be believed.'

James sat down and began to tell Anna all about his day, how Harriet had been turned back into a young girl and about flying over the hills, the tour of the caverns and Harriet's fright in the black lagoon.

Anna listened intently; she could tell by James's enthusiasm that it was all true. James was not one for romancing or spinning a yarn.

'I would love to meet them; do you think they would agree to it?' asked Anna.

'If you like we'll have a walk up there tomorrow, they know all about you and Harriet has told them that you're a good friend of hers. Tommy did say he would like to meet you, so I think there's a good chance they will appear if there's no one else about. What do you say?'

'I would love that. I'm sorry I shouted at you when you came home, but I was worried', said Anna.

'Let's not say any more about it, let's just look forward to tomorrow', said James.

The morning could not come quickly enough for Anna; she was trying her best to keep her excitement under control. James had a good idea that something was playing on Anna's mind. For a start, it wasn't very often that Anna was up before him, but she was today.

'What's the matter? Could you not sleep?' asked James.

Anna had brought James a cup of tea up to bed. This was a rare event.

'No, I've hardly slept all night. I didn't think I would be so excited about meeting your Trogglybogs, but I just can't wait. Do you think they will show themselves to me?' asked Anna.

'I don't see why not, after all I have told them all about you and so has Harriet, and they trust Harriet completely – and I think they trust me now!' James said with a wry sort of grin on his face.

'Right then, when are we going?' enquired Anna.

She was like a little girl about to set off on a day out to the seaside. She was now bouncing up and down on the bed and spilling James's tea all over. James could see he wasn't to be allowed a lie-in this morning. He put his cup down and headed for the shower.

'You can make me another cup of tea, seeing the bed got that one', shouted James from the bathroom. After his shower James quickly dressed and was beginning to get just as excited as Anna about the prospect of introducing his wife to his newfound friends. On his way downstairs the smell of bacon greeted him; Anna had cooked them both a hearty breakfast.

'My! You are on the ball this morning', exclaimed James. 'Not that I'm complaining, mind! I'd better just give the dogs a quick run before we set off.'

Both dogs heard James and they knew his every word; soon the tails were wagging and they were looking up at their leads in anticipation.

'I can't say anything, those two know every word', said James, shaking his head.

'You take the dogs and I'll go to the shop and buy some sweets. Well, I can't go up there without some kind of a present, can I?'

James had to smile, after all the earache Anna had given him for buying so many sweets, but he knew her intentions were right and the sweets would be just the sort of friendly gesture the Trogglybogs would like.

James took the dogs to the field and gave them a good run around, throwing their toys for them until his arm was aching.

'OK boys, that's your lot for now. Come on – I'll take you for a long walk later.' James picked up the dogs' ball and rubber ring and headed for home. Anna was all ready with her walking boots on, and the sweets were in James's rucksack.

'I've made us some tea in a flask and packed some chocolate biscuits and crisps as well. Do you think I should make some sandwiches?' asked Anna.

'No way, we've only just had breakfast. How long are you planning on stopping up on the moors?' laughed James.

James picked up the rucksack and off they went. The village

was quite busy for this early on a Saturday. James looked at his watch; it was only 8am. The postman was on his rounds and as they walked down the village PC Hoyle was just coming out of the newsagents.

'Good morning you two, looks like you're off out for the day.'

'Good morning Peter', said James. 'We're going for a nice stroll on the moors … it looks like it's going to be a beautiful day for a walk up there.'

'Yes it certainly does. Mind the Trogglybogs don't get you!' said PC Hoyle, laughing.

James looked at Anna, and they both burst out laughing too. 'If only he knew!' they both thought.

It was a lovely walk up the lane and onto the moors; the sun was shining and was already quite warm. The trees were all full of leaves now and the colours were stunning in the early morning sun. It was as if all the animals in the woods were telling each other that spring had finally arrived; the noise from the birds and insects was incredible.

It only took James and Anna twenty minutes to reach the top of the lane. Before going through the gate and onto the moors, James turned and looked back out across the valley towards the village.

'Just look at that view, there's no nicer place to be on a day like today.'

Anna agreed, the view was beautiful.

'C'mon, let's go and find them', said James, opening the gate for Anna.

'Where do you think they will be?' asked Anna; her eyes were scouring the hills as far and as fast as she could.

'Don't you worry about them, they will probably know we're here already and I'm pretty sure they will show themselves when they're ready.'

James and Anna walked on towards Great Hill. The path that leads that way passes a long row of shooting butts that are used by the grouse shooters in August. As James was looking around for his friends, he spotted Harry the fox.

James called to Harry to come over.

'Harry, come here. It's all right, this is Anna, my wife. I told you I would bring her.'

Harry was a good one hundred yards away from James and Anna. He sat there and nodded his head up and down. No sooner had James shouted this than one stick after another came flying over the top of the shooting butts.

James began to laugh and Anna smiled knowingly.

'They're here, aren't they?' Anna asked James.

'Yes, I do believe they are', said James as he ducked the sticks.

'OK, I know it's you! You can come out. I've brought Anna to meet you and she's brought you some sweets.'

As soon as James mentioned the sweets, that was it. First to break cover was little Tosh, followed by Lily. Tommy jumped up on top of the shooting butt and stood there, hands on hips like the true leader that he was.

'Welcome Anna. Harriet and James say we can trust you. Can we?'

Tommy's tone was very matter-of-fact. He needed to be sure that he could trust Anna before he would allow himself to relax.

'Thank you, and I promise you that you can trust me. I will never betray you; you have my word.'

Anna meant what she said; she was clearly overcome with the sight of these small lovable beings she had just met for the first time. By now Tosh was all over James, searching his pockets for sweets.

'If you're looking for sweets, Anna has them in the rucksack.'

Anna bent down and opened the bag and proceeded to hand out all the sweets. Tommy just stood on top of the shooting butt and stared at Anna. James walked over to him and asked what was wrong.

'I sense something about Anna, she's different from you and Harriet, and anyone else we've met up here for a long time. It's nothing bad, just something different', said Tommy.

James shook his head; he had never seen Tommy as serious

as this before and it was clear to James that Tommy would not relax until he had got to the bottom of whatever it was that was so different about Anna. James called Anna over to talk to Tommy.

'Tommy is puzzled, he thinks there is something different about you, but he doesn't know what it is', explained James.

'Really … well I don't know what it could be, but I do promise you, Tommy, that you can trust me and I won't harm or betray your trust', said Anna.

'No it's nothing like that. I feel as if I know you already, but I know I don't, it's so strange', said Tommy.

'Wait … I remember Harriet telling us that your name used to be Rigby!

My maiden name was Rigby – perhaps there's a connection? Perhaps I'm a distant relative. My family has always lived in the village', said Anna.

'That might be it', smiled Tommy, 'I just know there's something about you that's different from everyone else I've met. That would be strange. I might be your great, great, great, great uncle!' Tommy began to laugh and then everyone else fell about, laughing uncontrollably at the thought of Tommy being Anna's uncle. By now Harry the fox had joined the party, and James called Harry over.

'Harry, I'd like you to meet my wife. Anna, this is Harry', said James, introducing the two.

Harry sat down and politely offered Anna his paw to shake. Anna was overjoyed at being able to shake hands – or paws as the case may be, with a real live fox.

'How do you do, Harry? James has told me all about you', said Anna.

Harry just sat and nodded his head in approval, and then Anna reached into the bag and produced a handful of dog biscuits for Harry.

'Well, I had half-hoped I would meet Harry', said Anna to James.

James smiled. Anna could be so considerate; he had no idea

that she had even thought about meeting Harry. The day went wonderfully well and although Anna didn't get to visit the caves that day, Tommy did promise that they would take her down there soon. James and Anna decided to stay on the moors for a while longer. Tommy and the rest of the Trogglybogs waved goodbye and disappeared as fast as they had appeared.

James and Anna sat on the hilltop and enjoyed the view; they drank their tea from the flask that Anna had brought, and ate their chocolate biscuits before setting off home. It was now almost half past one – how quickly those few hours had flown. Anna had enjoyed herself more than she could ever have imagined. She had played games with some of the little ones and had shook hands with a fox. The only sad thing was, she knew she would never be able to speak to anyone about her experiences.

⚐ 10 ⚑

The Casket

With the excitement of the week's holiday now behind him, it was back to work for James. All the usual questions came his way.

'How was your holiday?' 'Did you go anywhere exciting?' 'What did you get up to?'

Of course James played it down; after all he couldn't very well tell his workmates that he'd spent the week on the moors flying through the air with 400-year-old hairy children, shaking hands with a fox and exploring an amazing underground world.

'Oh you know, the usual – decorating, and walking the dogs, nothing too exciting', replied James, with his fingers crossed.

James arrived home from work late in the afternoon and was met by Bracken and Skip. He could always be sure of a warm welcome from those two, even if it was only because they wanted a biscuit. James gave the dogs their biscuits and made the usual fuss. He could see Anna out in the back garden and he went out to join her.

'Hi, how was your first day back?' Anna enquired.

'Oh you know, just the usual, nothing exciting!' replied James. 'It was so hard not to tell the lads what I had really got up to, but I would probably have been taken away in a straitjacket if I had, so I told them I'd been decorating.'

Anna laughed. 'I know what you mean; I wish I could tell someone, but we both know we can't ... and we mustn't, ever!'

James nodded his head, he helped Anna to pick up the

rubbish that she'd collected in the garden, and then he called to the dogs.

'C'mon you two, let's get your leads. I'll take them out now', he said to Anna. 'I'll call round by Harriet's, just to see if she's all right.'

James picked up the dogs' leads, and the dogs were at the door before him, barking at one another in their usual impatient way. James opened the door and off down the path they ran, barking all the way until they got to the gate. James caught up with them there and put them both on their leads. The two dogs were not allowed off the lead until they were well away from the traffic. Brinscall was only a village, but the roads were quite busy.

After the dogs had been for their walk through the woods, James headed down by the waterfall and past the trout fishery towards the disused railway crossing; Harriet's cottage was just at the other side of the crossing. James liked to go past the trout lake very quietly; he had often seen deer in the woods just there by the lakeside.

He had always meant to take his camera with him when he intended to go that way, but on the odd occasion he'd remembered it, he didn't see any. Today was no exception, James looked in all the places he had seen them in the past, but there were no deer to be seen this afternoon. The only wildlife around were the grey squirrels, which were busy foraging for food.

The dogs bounded over the crossing, but James took his time. The dogs were always twenty yards in front – it was hardly any wonder the deer were not to be seen with these two lively hounds on the loose. Once they were across it was only a few yards to Harriet's house. James called the dogs back and put them on their leads. He opened the gate and tied the two dogs to the fence.

'You two stay there and be good; I won't be long', said James, giving the dogs a biscuit each.

As he walked towards the door he saw Harriet at the far end

of her garden, sitting on her bench. As he got closer he could see she was crying.

'What on earth's the matter? Have you fallen?' he asked her.

'No,' she sobbed, 'nothing like that, but something very frightening has happened to me', she told him.

'Let's get you inside and you can tell me all about it', said James.

James helped the frail old lady to her feet and took her inside the cottage; he sat her down and went to make some tea. After putting the kettle on, he sat down beside her. She was still crying, but very relieved that James had come round. Slowly she calmed down and was just about to tell James what it was that had upset her when the whistle on the kettle blew. James went into the kitchen and made the tea.

'Right, now then what has got you into such a state?' he asked.

Still sobbing, Harriet told James that she believed she had been visited by the ghost of her late mother, but before she could explain she burst into floods of tears. James calmed her down again and told her not to worry, just to tell him what had happened.

'I had gone to bed at my usual time last night and had fallen asleep after I had read my book for a while. I must have been asleep for about two or three hours when I felt as if someone was sat on my bed. The feeling of heaviness on my feet woke me with a start.

I reached for my lamp, but it wouldn't work – that's the first time in fifty years it has not worked! I rubbed my eyes and called out – "Is there someone there?"

There was no answer, but I could see in the shadows of the room, a dark figure of a woman dressed in a black cape, with a hood, just like the one my mother used to wear. Then slowly a mist appeared around the figure. By now I was quite frightened, then the woman spoke and I knew it was my mother even though I hadn't heard her voice for over sixty years. But she was different, she had an evil tone in her voice.

She told me I had to finish the task she had begun: she said there is a casket buried in my garden at the foot of the old yew tree; she said that inside the casket were the instructions of what I was to do.'

Harriet started to sob again; James put his arms around her.

'Come on, I'm sure it was just a bad dream', said James as he tried to reassure her.

'This was no dream, this was real. After she disappeared my light came on and my cat was going frantic trying to get out of the bedroom. No, believe me, this was real!'

'Very well, I'll take the dogs home and I'll come back with my spade, and we'll see if there is a casket beneath the yew tree.'

James gave Harriet another hug and by the time he had finished his tea, she had stopped crying. James told Harriet about Anna's visit to the moors, and how she had met with Harry the fox and shook paws with him. This helped to cheer her up and soon she was laughing at James's tales.

James gave her another hug and then was on his way down the path to where the two dogs were waiting. He turned, waved and was on his way. Fifteen minutes later he was walking into the house, just as Anna was about to serve the tea.

'Can mine wait? I've just left Harriet and she's a bit upset, I need to get my spade and go back down there.'

Anna asked what was the matter with Harriet and James told her all about it, and that he thought it was probably nothing more than a bad dream. Anna agreed with him, but she insisted on going back with him, just to keep Harriet company. James grabbed his spade from the shed and put it into the back of his car.

As they arrived at Harriet's cottage she was at the front door ready to greet them, and although she was smiling, Anna could tell that she was clearly upset. Once inside it was the usual ritual; tea first, talk after. Harriet tried to put a brave face on the whole thing and was asking Anna about her experience on the moors. Anna told her she'd had a wonderful time and soon they were having a good laugh. James decided this was a good time to go outside and start digging.

The old yew tree that Harriet had at the bottom of her garden was hundreds of years old. The cottage was dated 1660 and James wondered if the tree had been planted around the same time. James began to dig. The soil was quite soft at the front of the tree, and soon James had dug down about three feet, it was then that he hit something hard. As he dug he uncovered a large flat stone, square in shape, and as big as a paving stone.

James dug some more and scraped the soil away, then he reached down and managed to lift the stone. Underneath he found a stone chamber and inside the chamber was indeed an old wooden casket. He stopped and looked at it, wondering if he should remove it or cover it back up again – if he was to let Harriet see the casket it might frighten her. He was unsure what to do for the best. Just then Harriet and Anna came up the path and now he had no choice – he had to show Harriet what he had found.

'There, I told you so! I told you it wasn't a dream. Right, bring it inside, and let's see what's inside it.' Harriet was quite pleased with herself; she had been proved right.

Once inside, Harriet placed some newspaper on the floor for James to put the casket on. It was locked with an old padlock; James went to his car and returned with a hammer and chisel. He knelt down at the side of the box, and placing the chisel on the lock, he asked Harriet if she was sure it was what she wanted.

'Yes, I need to know what that casket holds, and what is so important as to make my mother haunt me like that after all these years. Why has she waited all this time? Why now?' asked Harriet.

James swung his hammer; the lock was so rusty that it snapped open on the first hit. He found the lid somewhat harder to open, as the hinges had become solid with time, but eventually James managed to prise it open. The three of them peered into the box.

Inside was a goblet, a bottle and a scroll. James picked up the scroll. It was tied with a piece of tatty lace that fell to pieces as James tried to untie it. James opened the scroll and looked at it for a moment, before asking Harriet if she wanted him to read it. She nodded.

'It's very hard to read … it's in old-style writing. Just give me a moment. You might not like what it says here – are you sure?' he asked Harriet.

'Yes, I'm sure; please read it', said Harriet.

James took a few minutes to look at the writing, it had become a little faded with time and the fact that it was in old-style script didn't help. When he had finished he turned to Harriet and told her that what was written here might shock her. Again he asked her if she was sure she wanted to know the contents of the scroll and again she nodded. Anna put her arm around Harriet and held her close as James told her what the scroll contained.

'It is indeed from your mother, and I'm sorry, I know this seems to be unbelievable, but it appears your mother was the old witch that laid the curse upon the Trogglybogs all those years ago. It also says that she wants you to finish off what she started. She explains that her curse went wrong and that she never meant for the Trogglybogs to live forever.

She goes on to say that she has waited until now because you now have friends that you can trust and that this should make it easier for you to do what you have to. Do you think she means Anna and me? She also talks about your father, but doesn't say who he was … there's also a rhyme.'

Harriet stopped James and asked to see the scroll. She put on her reading glasses and began to study the writing, occasionally stopping to ask James what a certain word said. It took her a while to read the message on the scroll, but by the time she had finished it was clear that she understood what it was her mother wanted from her. Harriet shook her head and began to cry. Anna held her close as James took the scroll from her, rolled it up and placed it back in the casket.

Dearest Daughter

I have waited until now for good reason to reveal all these long kept secrets to you. I feel now assured that you have trusted friends about you. Friends who can assist you to end the work that I began many years ago.

In November of the year 1602 AD. I was cruelly treated by the folk who dwelled upon the moors and in the valleys around about. I took it on myself to punish all those who had treated me so. I cursed them all, condemning their children to a life underground. It was my desyre to have them be troglodytes, and to live in caves forever.

Alas, my curse was spoken wrongly, and today they are still living. They are growing stronger all the time because of the magic powers they now have. Then I hatched a plan that I knew would one day see the end of these cursed creatures. I found a man of good breeding who would produce me a good strong offspring. Who he was, is of no matter.   Once you were born my daughter, I rid myself of that man.

Now that you have your friends, you must go onto the moors and destroy all the creatures that I created. Once they are gone, then I can rest in peace forever. Here is what you must do.

You must drink the wine from the chalice and repeat the rhyme three times.

Be free, be free, be free of me
Drink the wine, be free of me
Those who drink will mighty be
And finish the dance for eternity.
Do it good daughter and enjoy my eternal gratitude.

Fail me at your peril..

'What do you want to do about this?' James asked Harriet.

It was clear to them all that it was the intention of the witch that Harriet should kill her beloved Trogglybogs, but Harriet would have none of that. There was no way she would dream of harming them, she had after all grown up with them, and loved them as her own.

'James, will you take the casket away and destroy it or whatever you think is best? Just take it a long way from here; I don't want to see it again.'

James agreed to do this for Harriet; he took the box out to his car and put it in the boot. Once it was out of the house Harriet seemed to be more at ease and began to relax a little.

'What do you want to do tonight? I mean will you be all right here on your own? You can always come and stay a night or two at our house if you feel you don't want to be alone', said Anna.

'Thank you, but I'll be fine; no ghost of an old witch is going to drive me out of my house.'

'I still can't understand it – if she was the witch in 1602, how could she be your mother just over three hundred years later?' asked a confused James.

'I don't know that either, but if she ever shows her face again, I'll be sure to ask her', replied Harriet.

11

The Witch's Revenge

James and Anna stayed for another cup of tea and the casket wasn't mentioned again. The rest of the evening was spent listening to Harriet's tales of the days she spent on the moors with the Trogglybogs, and the stories they had told her of events over the course of their lives. They had seen and been involved in all kinds of adventures, including the English Civil War. They had also assured Harriet that UFOs and aliens really do exist.

'You must ask Tommy about that next time you see him; he will open your eyes', said Harriet.

James said he would. It had now gone ten o'clock and James had to be up early for work the next day. Anna again asked Harriet if she would be all right on her own. Harriet assured her she would, and the two of them gave her a goodnight kiss. James said he would call round to see her tomorrow after work.

'James, promise me that you will not allow the witch and her evil curse to make you bring any harm to the Trogglybogs – please promise me!' pleaded Harriet.

'Don't you worry about that, I would never harm them', assured James.

As James and Anna left they could hear Harriet bolting her door.

'All the bolts in the world are not going to keep out the witch', James said to Anna.

'No, but she still needs to make sure her house is safe, living all that way down there on her own', said Anna.

The following day James went to work and Anna decided to

have a walk down to Harriet's to see if she'd had any more unwelcome visits, but Harriet was pleased to say she hadn't. Harriet was curious to know what James had done with the casket.

'As far as I know, it's still in the boot of his car. I don't think he's decided what to do with it yet, but he did say that he might bury it on Pendle Hill; he joked that it might be at home there with Pendle's witch history!'

Harriet chuckled at the thought, but also agreed that it would make her happy – the further away it was, the better. Later, as Anna walked home, she looked across towards the woods and the moors beyond. She wondered if the Trogglybogs' magic would be strong enough to destroy the casket and its contents. Harriet's mother, the witch, had a great deal of power. Anyone who could do what she had done and then return to life again after all these years by such strange means, was dangerous and could not be treated lightly;

Anna was a little afraid and wondered what they had got themselves into.

James arrived home at the usual time and was just about to sit down to read his newspaper when there was a knock at the door. Anna answered it.

'James, it's Tom, you had better come here quickly!' shouted Anna.

James could tell by the tone of Anna's voice that something was very wrong and he dashed to the door.

'James, you're a friend of old Miss Bond, aren't you?' asked Tom.

'You had better get down there fast – her house is on fire! PC Hoyle is down there and the fire brigade has been called, but it doesn't look too good for her, the house is well alight.'

Tom was shaking; he had run all the way from the Hall. James grabbed his car keys and he and Anna rushed out of the house. As James drove down the lane past the big Hall, he could see Harriet's cottage ablaze and out of the smoke rose a sight that made James brake hard.

'Look at that – can you see it?' James asked Anna.

'Good heavens! What is it?' said Anna.

Rising out of the smoke, James and Anna could both see the face of the old witch, her eyes piercing as she stared straight at them. The smoke swirled and rose high into the afternoon sky. The witch's face rose with it, distorting as it went. Then the image appeared to say something, laughed and finally disappeared.

James and Anna were both shocked and scared. James looked at Anna and then drove on to Harriet's cottage, and their first concern was their friend. James parked the car out of the way of the fire engines which were also just arriving.

James ran over to where PC Hoyle was. He had managed to pull Harriet away from the burning building, and was giving her first aid.

'How is she, Peter?' James asked.

'Not too good I'm afraid, she's got one or two burns, but she's inhaled a lot of smoke. The ambulance is on its way'.

When the ambulance arrived, Anna agreed to go to the hospital with Harriet and James followed in his car. Harriet was unconscious all the way to hospital; the ambulance man was giving her oxygen and treating her burns all the way there.

When they arrived Harriet was taken for emergency treatment and a nurse came to ask Anna and James for some details. They were told they would be able to see Harriet as soon as the doctors had treated her. They waited and waited. It was only an hour, but it seemed like a day before the doctor came out to speak to them.

The doctor suggested they go somewhere a little quieter. 'This doesn't sound too good', thought James. The doctor took them into a side office and began to explain to them what injuries Harriet had. James's fears were well founded; the news was not good.

'I'm afraid your friend is very poorly. She has inhaled a lot of smoke and due to her age her lungs are not strong enough to recover from such damage. We have got her comfortable for

now and you may see her if you like, but I must warn you, I cannot see her surviving the night', said the doctor.

Anna was very upset and James put his arm around her.

'Thank you doctor, we would like to see her please. Is she awake?' asked James.

'She is drifting in and out of consciousness. Try not to tire her, she is very weak', said the doctor.

James and Anna were shown into a side ward. Harriet was propped up with an oxygen mask over her face to help her breathe. She looked so small and frail in the bed. They both sat down and Anna took hold of Harriet's hand. After a few minutes Harriet opened her eyes and asked where her cat was, James assured her he would find it and take care of it until she was well again. Harriet smiled; she looked at them both and removed the mask.

'We both know I'm not going to get well, James, but if my cat is all right, please will you take care of her for me? She's been a good friend to me.' Harriet could hardly speak and James could only just make out what she was trying to say.

'Try not to speak, you will need all your strength', James told her, but Harriet was having none of it; she had to give James some last instructions.

'James, this was no accident … it was the witch's revenge for me not obeying her wishes. You must be very careful; she is a very dangerous witch. Speak to Tommy; he may be able to help you, but whatever you do, you must warn him that the witch is back … they are in grave danger!' Harriet began to get worked up and James put the mask back on her face, Anna called for the nurse.

The nurse called the doctor and James and Anna were asked to wait outside. After a few minutes the doctor came out; it was clear from the look on his face that all was not well.

'I'm very sorry, but Miss Bond has died', said the doctor. 'You can go in and see her if you like.'

Both Anna and James were upset, but said they would like a few moments alone with their friend. Harriet looked very peaceful, and appeared to have a slight smile on her face. James stood and promised Harriet that he would do all he could to protect Tommy and all the others. He also knew that it would be very difficult to have to go onto the moors and break the news of Harriet's death to them, but there was no one else to do it.

The following day, James rang work and explained to his boss what had happened. Stuart was very understanding and told James to take as long as he needed.

The following day James got up at 5am, although he had been awake for most of the night trying to work out what to do with the casket and how to break the news of Harriet's death to Tommy and the other Trogglybogs. James decided to take the casket and bury it miles from the village. He had thought of destroying it, but something in his mind told him that it might be better to hide it for now.

James told Anna what he was going to do, but wouldn't tell her where he was going to hide the casket; he thought it better if she didn't know. He remembered Harriet telling him that her mother had come from the Pendle area, so he made up his mind that was were he would bury the casket, somewhere on the side of Pendle Hill.

The drive to Pendle took an hour and as James stood on the very top of the hill, he could see the hills of Brinscall in the distance. He took his spade out of the boot and walked down the hill until he found a place where he couldn't be seen from the road and began to dig. He dug down about four feet, then he went back to the car for the casket.

Once the job was done, James sat in his car for a while. It was now lunchtime. Next he faced the worst task of the day. He had to go onto the moors and break twenty-four little hearts. Anna had said she would go with him and he knew he would need all the help and support he could get that afternoon.

It was a beautiful afternoon and the spring sunshine was warm, but James knew that a great cloud was going to descend on Brinscall moors that day. The walk up to the top of the hill wasn't rushed; it was a walk neither James nor Anna wanted to take. They were both nervous and even though James had thought of nothing else all day, he still hadn't any idea how he would break his news.

They walked through the gate and made their way over the track, past the shooting butts, eventually arriving at the crossroads where the path goes down to White Coppice, but there was no sign of any of the Trogglybogs. James suggested they walk down the valley to the place where he first made contact with them. When they arrived at the spot, they sat on the grass and James shouted out Tommy's name.

'Good afternoon', said a voice behind them.

James and Anna looked round to see Tommy and Lily standing there; almost immediately they were joined by Tosh and half a dozen of the others.

'Have you brought us some sweets?' asked little Tosh, who was told to shut up by Tommy.

'Is that all you think about? Sweets!' said Tommy.

'Its all right Tommy, but no I haven't brought any sweets this time. I'm afraid I have some very bad news', said James.

Tommy looked at them both and he knew right away what the bad news was.

'It's Harriet, isn't it? What's happened to her? Please don't tell us she's died', pleaded Tommy.

James put his arms around Tommy and Anna did the same with the others. Their little bodies shook with the upset and tears were shed by everyone, including James and Anna.

Tommy calmed himself enough to suggest they go into the caves. This they all did and once inside James told them everything that had happened, including what Harriet had told him about the witch being her mother. Tommy wondered if opening the dark cavern had released the old witch from her age-old prison. After all it was only after Harriet had been in there that things had started to happen.

James had even wondered if he was to blame in any way; after all, it was also only after he had become involved with the Trogglybogs too; but Tommy would have none of it. All of them agreed with Tommy, but there was still doubt in James's mind.

'First, we must block off the dark cavern completely, secondly we will go to the Saxon cavern and speak to the spirit leader, he will help us and tell us what to do', said Tommy, who had now become very calm and was in complete control.

'I will go back to the place where I buried the casket, dig it up and burn it; so it can't do any more harm to anyone', said James.

James had also made up his mind that he would not be involving himself with the Trogglybogs any more, as he couldn't help but blame himself for what had begun since he came into their lives. He gathered them all around and explained to them how he felt; he told them that he would always be there for them, but only when they really needed him.

'I will still come onto the moors and I will leave sweets for you so you don't need to worry about that', he said, looking at little Tosh. 'And if you ever need me for anything you only have to ask, but I think it's for the best if I don't see you so often. If that witch has any hold over me, I don't want her to be able to use me to get to you.'

Tommy and the others were upset at the thought of not seeing James, but Tommy understood and thanked James.

'We will see you from time to time, won't we?' enquired little Tosh.

'Of course you will, but we must distance ourselves ... for a while at least!' said James.

'Right, there is work to be done. We must block off the dark cavern right away', said Tommy.

'Yes, and I must go and destroy the casket', said James.

James and Anna gave big hugs to everyone and then left. They climbed the hill out of Devil's Valley and once at the top they looked back to see all their friends waving to them. James wondered if he would ever enter the caverns again. Anna took his hand and they walked off. On their way home they went by Harriet's cottage – what a mess it was! The roof had fallen in and smoke was still rising from the smouldering building.

PC Hoyle was standing in the garden holding something in his hands. When James got closer he could see that it was the remains of Harriet's magic lamp.

'What have you there, Peter?' asked James.

'I don't know what it is, but it's amazing! Just look at this, if you touch the stone it lights up, and if you touch it again, it goes out.'

'That was Harriet's magic lamp. I don't know how it works either, I used to always be messing with it when I came round here – she said I could have it when anything happened to her, but I never thought it would be so soon, or as nasty as this', said James.

Peter passed the lamp to James, and just as he did, Harriet's cat came out of the bushes meowing and snuggling her head into Anna's legs.

'Looks like you've got something else to take home with you as well as a magic lamp. If you ever find out how that thing works, let me know, will you?' said Peter.

Anna picked up the cat and they went home, wondering how the two dogs would react to a cat moving in with them: they had never had a cat before. Once in the house Anna held Harriet's cat firmly in her arms, then James brought the two dogs into the room. At first the dogs were very excited that James and Anna had arrived home, but as soon as they saw the cat they stopped in their tracks and walked slowly over to Anna. The cat's back rose up and she began to hiss at the two dogs, but the dogs just sniffed at the cat and began to wag their tails. Anna put the cat down on the floor and soon all three of them were getting on quite well, although the cat was soon putting Bracken in his place after he started to get a little too playful.

The next morning James decided to go back to Pendle to dig up the casket. He put his spade in the boot of the car and was off. He found the spot where he had parked two days earlier and grabbed his spade, and walked down the hill to where the casket was buried, looking around all the time to make sure no one was about. He jumped over the wall where the casket was buried and almost fell into a huge hole.

The casket was gone: someone had dug it up before him. This set James's mind racing. Had someone seen him bury it? Or had the witch got it? What was James going to tell Anna and Tommy?

Perhaps it would be better to say nothing to Tommy and the rest of the Trogglybogs. After all, there was no point in worrying them – it might just have been someone with a metal detector out looking for buried treasure. But what if they drank the wine and repeated the rhyme? They might turn into something like the witch.

James had to stop himself from thinking all these thoughts. He decided the best thing to do was to go home, tell Anna what had happened, but say nothing to the Trogglybogs.

James arrived home and calmly walked in. He took his spade out to the shed and put it away before saying anything to Anna.

'Well, have you burned the casket?' she asked.

'Not exactly – it wasn't there!' replied James.

James told Anna the whole story; how he went to the spot where he had buried the casket but only found an empty hole. Anna was as mystified as he was, but agreed with James that they should say nothing to the Trogglybogs about its disappearance.

All that day they spoke about nothing else, and in the end James said they should try and put the whole business of the casket behind them and not worry about something that they could do nothing about. Just before going to bed, James took the dogs into the back garden as usual. Anna was left to turn off the television and put the lights out.

James was standing at the back door looking up at the stars, when Anna called to him in a very calm voice that had a sense of urgency about it.

'James – can you come here please – quickly?'

James walked back into the house – Anna was in the doorway of the lounge, staring into the room.

'What is it? What's the matter?' he asked.

As James reached Anna, the lights were out in the room, but he could tell by the look on Anna's face that there was something very wrong. She was shaking. She pointed into the lounge, and in the corner of the room there was a strange grey mist rising from the floor to the ceiling. James immediately remembered Harriet describing a grey mist in her bedroom.

Within seconds the mist was swirling and turning, then distorting, and out of the haze, sure enough appeared the image of the witch. She began to speak, but not as the evil old woman James had expected her to be; she was calm and relaxed.

'My daughter is dead and now I must find someone else who is of the same bloodline as I, to take upon themselves the task that I failed. Until then, you must be the guardians of the casket. Do not try to destroy it or discard it – you cannot! My power will not allow it to happen. I will return for the casket soon'.

Before the witch disappeared, James called to her –

'Wait … why is it so important to you to kill the children of the moor? They can do you no harm, and why did you have to kill your own daughter?'

The witch gasped and the mist swirled even faster.

'How dare you question me? But since you dare to ask.

They have to die, because I cannot rest in my grave until they are gone. The night I laid my curse upon them I slipped and fell to my death, down a deep and long tunnel that led into a dark and watery grave. I didn't have the chance to finish and now they will live forever, unless I can find someone of the same bloodline as myself, who can end this madness.

As for my daughter, she was not my real daughter. I stole her from someone who was of the same bloodline and until she was grown I cared for her as my own, but she was weak, just like all the others!

Soon I will find the right person, and then everything will be done and I will be able to rest.'

Before James had the chance to say anything else the witch and the mist disappeared. Anna switched on the light and at the same time James's attention was drawn to the two dogs who were barking furiously. James went to the back door to see what was going on, and there on the lawn was the casket.

James stayed up that night and buried the casket in his garden. He buried it deep and covered it with two large old stone flags that had been leaning against the wall.

'Well, it looks like Tommy and Co are safe for the time being, until the witch finds someone who's of the same bloodline as herself. Then it will probably start all over again', he said to Anna.

All he and Anna could do now was wait and see what happened next.

THE END